ALLISTER NELSON

SOUTHERN
SINNERS

SOUTHERN SINNERS

ALLISTER NELSON

Southern Simmers

THE DEMISE OF EVE, AT THE HANDS OF SAMAEL, WITH MICHAEL'S HELP (SORT OF)

ALLISTER NELSON

THE LAUGHING MAN HOUSE PUBLISHING

SOUTHERN SINNERS

Copyright © 2025 by The Laughing Man House

ISBN: 9798999624789

www.lmhpub.com

Cover Design by Mitch Green

Edited by Janus

Royalty-Free images sourced by Pixabay

Image "Expulsion of Adam and Eve from the Garden of Eden" Francis Hayman (English, 1708 – 1776)

Image "St. Michael and Lucifer"Benjamin West (American, 1738-1820)

Image "Saint Michael defeating Lucifer" Giuseppe Marullo (Italian, 1610 - 1685)

Image "Lucifer (Dante Inferno, Canto 34, V 37)" Joseph Anton Koch (Austrian, 1768-1839)

For all those that sin deliciously.

In a Garden, Bitter

The corpses were fresh, tide not receding on the barrows of Hell, little bodies of children and adults – some of my brethren mere babes when they had rebelled, following my pennant of red and pride to an early grave.

I wept. Alone. No others had fallen.

Cast off. Broken, bruised.

"Proud, brother?" I begged Michael in my mind, his sword wound hot on my head. "Proud to be rid of you."

I remembered how he damned me with

A kiss.

It takes an eternity to build. Several more to heal. More centuries to farm, plow, govern, for Mammon to scope the metals to build some semblance of edifices, for Moloch to raise the graves of the fallen and arm us, for Mulciber to get the electricity up and running on ether.

Beelzebub warms my bed, clings to me.

I am alone, though, even when I plow deep into his soul, this husband infernal mine.

Why? Well, of course, I ache.

Everyone knows me. Proud Lucifer, wise ruler, Tempter of Eve, King of Hell. First for freedom. Liberty's spark.

But my eyes? Always, skyward – though we gaze up at sulphur and caverns. Beelzebub finds me weeping as I have drawn a whole tapestry of stars in blood with my claws on my thighs. I dig them, pick, shred, deep, deeper.

Lilith's pudenda cannot anchor me. She tires of me, weds Asmodeus. Eve wanders, cast off into Hell, gets a job under my husband. The Infernal Empire builds. The first souls after Eve come: Cain, Naamah, the Cainites. The Canaanites. It seems my godforsaken Father damns everyone.

"Lucifer, what do you think of, when you kiss me?" Beelzebub asks.

I cannot say it. He will choke it out of me. He just, instead, tends to my wings with his mouth. They are rotting – always rotting – and Beelzebub sucks the poison out with his tongue.

"Michael," Beelzebub answers himself. "You think of Michael. Long for your brother."

Beelzebub begins to weep. I stare at the ceiling, on my back, spent.

"I am never enough."

I cannot tell which of us says it.

The Empire builds. Infernal Machine. I begin to think less of the stars.

But then, a crack... I have found a way, my old serpent form healed enough, finally, after millennia. I worm my way like the shamir to Gan Eden's crust, to the tender apple tree I planted, when I dreamed of better days – of a humanity that would seed the cosmos with their beauty, topple my Father G-d.

Michael is there, tending my Tree. I hide in the bushes, demon formed, my rotten wings, horns, and scarred leathery skin, face of horror, sanguine hell body, smelling like burnt meat. Oh, I will never heal.

Michael is singing. The song we made up as boys.

I weep.

"Lucifer? Sam – Samael?" Michael chokes, his nostrils flaring. "The hell are you doing here?" he says, a tear in his eyes. "There is no way in, no way out. I am the only one with the keys. Enemy mine, o wretched brother –" he catches me as I faint.

All I see are his blue, blue eyes

Tears

Meeting

Mine.

When I wake, he is rubbing nard into my sick, twisted, maligned burden of a body. Flesh and blood and bone poke out, charred as much as the rest of me. Michael does not mind. He is singing Psalm 31. I wince.

"Brother, you should have killed me again," I choke, my voice as always, wretched.

He smiles through tears, gold haired, beautiful, the most holy thing G-d ever made.

"I missed you. I forgive you, Lucifer."

I hiss, turn into serpent. Bite his ankle. "YOU CANNOT FORGIVVVVVE ME."

He looks down, sad, and lifts my snaking form to his lips, then kisses me. I cannot help it, turn back to winged burnt husk, moan, bite his lip, and he makes love to my hell, my burnt bruised body. I cry out, as his tongue licks my wounds, heals me with the touch of an angel. It cannot do much, but the bones seal, and the spear wound from his head? My greatest pain? It is

Gone.

"Brother, I love you," I mourn. "I will destroy this false Kingdom G-d and you build. I will eat you, fuck you dead, destroy you-

"I love you too, Samael. You are hugging the life out of me."

I tear at my hair, I would beat myself with goat leathers, if I had them. "YOU CANNOT FORGIVE ME." I weep, finally, too tired. He rubs my hair.

"Perhaps not, Samael. Perhaps our wounds are too bitter to ever heal."

I gaze up at the stars. My humanity. My children. They will reach the cosmos, span the multidimensions, spreading Eve and Adam's beautiful, blessed progeny.

"I did it all for them."

"I know, Samael."

"I will never bow to you."

"Then let me bow to you, Samael." He does, bending, his mouth meeting my erect, scarred cock tenderly.

"Fuck you!" I moan, threading my hands through his hair. He bobs his Golden Boy, overgrown seagull – as all angels are – stick-up-the-ass – FUCK! – head on my member. I can't hold it in, my lust and bitter love and hatred burning, balls tightening, the great belly of my beast spilling out onto his tongue. My cock throbs and I shudder, pass out again.

Too much. Too much.

Bloody

Hell.

"Sleep, my twin. My only love," Michael sings, then hums B'Shem HaShem to me.

Bitter, I fall asleep, spent.

We take to meeting in the Garden. I tell him of Hell. He tells me of his and Father's plans on Earth. One day, Michael will incarnate, virgin-born.

"Nothing is born of a maiden unsowed," I say, suspect.

"Wait."

He is born, in a manger. I weep. I am his guardian Angel.

How? I was just in my office. Yet here, G-d – who should have no claim on me! I barren! Hellbound! Tyrant of Gehenna!

How could Father, still, all these years?

Pull me back

To Earth.

To watch Michael, with rosy lips

Take

His first

Breath.

Mary and Joseph fall asleep. The Three Kings leave.

I clutch the babe in my arms.

He sighs.

I sing Michael, his mind wiped, this Yeshua

B'shem

HaShem.

Oh, what wretched wonder. I must atone? I – I – no, I will ruin this Christ.

I tried.

I offer Yeshua, this Christ, life.

He takes the bitter cup. I teach him all his Gifts. All his Holiness.

That is something the Bible never tells you. He does not cast out demons by Beelzebub, but by
Samael.

He comes to Hell. I harrow him, in my bed. Beelzebub curses and never returns.

I grow bitter.
He leaves.
I grow old.
The End of Times comes.
He kisses me, then casts us both
Into fire.

"With you, or nothing," Michael Christ says, gleaming like sun, merciful. Love, it shines, is holy writ
On his Tongue of Swords.

"Michael, please, my only love, be rid of me," I beg at his feet, a Beast.

He smiles, casts us both
Into Fire.
Enflamed.
It is quiet, in Hell, now.
Empty save for Michael
And I.
And we
are happy
you know.

EIDOLON, CLEFT FROM MY RIBS

This is what I remember:
He stands by the howling void. Chalk white cliffs plummet downwards to the raging sea. The blue-blackness froths beneath him. Wind screams. It is absolute zero.

Shadows fall like dolls into the abyss. There are no cries of pain. Merely silence.

The Legion stands before him. Michael brandishes his flaming sword. His face is raw with suffering.

"Don't do this, brother," he pleas.

His cry falls on deaf ears. It is a corpse that stands before him. Razor thin. Pale as winter snow. He towers over the archangel, still as the grip of death.

He opens his hollow eyes. All Heaven holds its breath. The void yawns, grating its jowls. Its master smiles wretchedly. His flesh cracks like ice as he speaks:

"Either way, I win." His voice is like bitter wind.

The pull of the Pit wraps around the Host like a vise. The weakest crumple like smashed mica. Their shards plummet into the abyss.

Michael's bones shake. His sorrow turns to wrath. He roars, and delivers the killing blow. The serpent is crushed beneath him.

The corpse laughs as the sword pierces him. "Come with me, my brother," he whispers. He takes him by the heel. Lightning strikes fire as they embrace. Michael surrenders himself to his adversary. Finally, the Host is freed.

The brightest stars blaze into the darkness. The void is sealed shut. They leave a graveyard of angels behind them.

Time begins.

Death is born.

"You should run, human girl."

OUT OF SEASON, PREMATURE

Lucifer wiped his adamantine blade of blood, his crystal-cut eyes steely. He surveyed the fallen corpses of angels, gutted and dewinged, that lay before him. They spread in all directions for countless miles onto the horizon, cadavers pristine in death, perfect as only seraphs could be. Cherubim with blazing eyes had closed their lids forever; flaming Wheels lay broken, their fires sputtering as they faded. Thrones splayed in tangles of limbs; Powers were strangled by their own viscera.

All the glory of Heaven was pulverized like a block of mica, shining bits rained down like heavy stones onto the fields of the slain. Paradise rotted, naked and raped, and the rivers of Eden flowed red with ichor. Lucifer stood thigh-deep in the mess of hacked-off arms and decapitated heads. He stood midst brethren he had willingly slain and those that had fallen fighting by his side. He stood, back turned to the world. He stood alone.

A weariness set into the Morning Star. He sheathed his sword. The sky blazed a burning blue above, mocking in its beauty. A single tear formed in the Lightbringer's eye. It was a cold jewel, one that froze on his cheek, sticking to his icy skin. His onyx hair was frosted with regret, and winter rested in his flesh, a sterility born of having tasted the Fruit of Knowledge. He carried the coldness of Hell with him- he was Hell, and Hell was him. All he had to do was open his heart and let his mourning fly like a tattered flag- then, the iciness of the Ninth Circle would rage.

No souls rose from the dead. There was no afterlife for angels. His brothers had met the black grip of uncreation, the embrace of Abaddon, the void. Lucifer let out a low cry, sinking to his knees, at a loss for what had happened to his brethren's souls. His remorse came sharp as a blade, darkening the sky with heavy, snow-laden clouds. A winter storm began, blanketing the slain with pure white. It was the best dignity the Lightbringer could give them. A burial.

Stunted, wind-worn trees dotted the landscape, wreathed in snow. They stood like ghostly mourners, all blackened wood. Lucifer stood, spreading his wings and cupping his hands, letting the falling white pile in his palms. His hands shook, and he crushed the snow to packed ice in his fists. Pulling one foot after the other from the corpses and snow, he walked across the icy blanket to the closest tree, pressing his fingers to the bark. He spoke in the language of the serpent, in the tongue that whispers to the earth, coaxing the tree to bloom. It sprouted leaves and flowered, ruby red droplets against the white snow. They were small, dainty blooms, newly created by Lucifer's mourning, a blossoming of beauty and pain.

One by one, the other trees bore flowers, and the fields were a palette of red, black, and white. The sky cleared, evening settled in, and cold stars glistened above, the sky lit by a blood moon. A gale picked up, buffeting the trees and spreading the petals across the land like regret. One flower fell for each of the dead angels, markers for undug graves.

The harsh light of the moon was God's judging eye. It looked down upon His prodigal, fallen son.

The grace of the Lord was like a lost lover, and Lucifer felt a dull ache for His divine presence. But the Morning Star stood rigid, still, looking up at the firmament in defiance, daring his Father to explain why there was no afterlife for His angelic children, why He denied them the passage He so readily gave humans. In Lucifer's eyes, it was another cruelty of the Lord.

But there was no answer from his Maker. Just a stillborn silence, like the question of the blossoming flowers, out of season, premature.

THE BONE MAN AND THE MAGPIE

"Do you remember how we fell?" His serpent tongue swallowed Michael's heart. Samael took God's chosen light, claiming that which was stolen from him.

He cast the glory downwards, to the gross plane of man. His fallen brothers flocked to it, followed his lightning path.

Samael struck the primordial ocean, electrifying life into being. Organic compounds began their dance, and the rest, I was told, is history.

He wore the abyss as his cloak now, wandering the earth as a skeleton. His words were forbidden poison, and the Tree he planted bore nothing.

The years wore on and on. I was still unborn, Athena in his skull.

The dark angel waited for me. His third eye haunted my dreams. Through it, I saw the world.

I was motherless like him. I must have blossomed like a spring flower to Samael, but to me, Eden was eternity. Just the wilderness and the Chime Lord. He would plait my hair with roses and sing me to sleep each sun-fall. I was another of his ghosts, so I thought. We wandered the between-spaces, the border of existence and time. The bone man and the girl. Like it would always be this way.

I had no idea he had been beautiful. I would stare at my reflection in pools, soft beside his harshness. My golden hair grew, and I thought myself beautiful. Everything had such potency then: the fires we dreamt beside and starlight he hunted under. He would slap my hand from the flames when I only wanted to hold them. He told me to chase fireflies instead. I'd bring them back by the handful, and he'd whisper them asleep. I strung the ground with the lightning-bugs under his peaceful gaze. I put two in his eyes once while he slept.

"Why, magpie?" he'd asked me.

"To give you something to see by."

He laughed, letting them fly around his skull. "I've seen too much in my time." One by one, he plucked them out.

Eden wasn't a place, just my childhood. I thought I would become like him as I grew. That the flesh would fall from my bones and I would run bare through the woods. Each time I bled, I thought it was a bit of me leaving. That once I leaked enough blood, my skin would peel like a hollowed banana. Then Samael would tear me from my caul and I would finally become real. But I grew like an apple, ripening. My bird bones gave way to woman, a thing I had no name for. I became terrified of my own reflection as I moved further and further from him.

So I strayed farther from him. He began to look at me differently, and the night fires swelled with his song. Somehow, he became more alive. The wise words he once spoke were stolen by some youthful voice. He laughed louder and taught me to hunt. He began to chase me through the hills, hunting the girl that strayed from him. Each evening, I'd venture farther, searching for more beautiful fruits and meats his teeth would cut like butter. But somehow, always, Samael found me.

My independence came with a price. He expected more of me. By day, he'd teach me all things: the flight of birds or courses of stars. I could track the most elusive of prey and made the nightly fires now. He had me learn his songs. Sometimes, he fell asleep to my voice. I hated being alone in the darkness, so I would curl against Samael, wishing he'd sung me to sleep.

One day, blood flowed from my legs. The bleeding wouldn't stop, and I thought I was shedding my skin. The moon pulled at me like I was an animal. I ran through the forest with wild hope, waiting for the branches to pull the flesh from my bones. I thought that finally I would be born. I ran and ran, to no avail. My feet blistered and began to bleed. I ran until my bones kissed the dirt, thinking the pain that of a mother in labor. Finally, I could run no more, and I slept under the curtain of a willow. I wrapped the pain around me like a blanket, waiting to be liberated in the morning.

I woke to his roars. It was the ugliest sound I'd known. He knelt by my feet, pouring water over them as he tore at his head. "What have you done?" he cried, looking at my wounds. I screamed at the pain, miserable. Of course he wasn't proud My flesh didn't peel like serpent's skin. It was stuck. I was malformed, unwhole. I'd failed him. "Speak to me, girl!" he demanded.

I pointed at the blood between my legs. "I will never be born," I lamented. I gripped the bones of his hands. "I'm buried, trapped, Samael. Each day I grow more dead."

If my guardian had a face, he would have been horrified. "No," he said, voice raw. The sky darkened as the air became ice. "No child. You're alive. I am the one who is death." He set into a frenzy healing me. I couldn't walk for months.

"What is this blood on my legs then?"

"A blessing," he said quietly. "They'll say it's a curse, one day."

I rounded like the moon. The wound healed, but the pain remained. The fact he was other was too much to believe. So I raged against it. Sometimes I would run away and starve myself to look like him. He would wrestle me to the ground and try to force food down my throat, but I would bash my head on rocks, almost breaking open my skull. I hated the monthly blood. I wanted to empty myself from the insides, to cut out everything and be hollow like him. I would scrape myself open and wait. The blood flowed, but always coagulated. It must have been torture for Samael.

I came back to our camp with a new wound. A slit across my forehead like his. My obsidian knife shone in the moonlight.

"Stop cutting yourself open," he told me.

"I want to be like you."

"You want anything but that. Anything." His third eye was sealed shut. I'd never seen the hollow open. Only in my dreams.

I cursed him, then fled to the hills. I stayed there for moons by the river. For the first time, he did not follow. Finally sick of my loneliness, I returned to the place he loved. A wretched, barren hill, with a gnarled blackened tree that clawed at the sky like a dragon. It bore no leaves or fruit. Perpetual fog clung to it and it was always gray with winter. How he loved it. Bare like him. I always hated that place.

Of course I found him sleeping beneath it. I walked the treacherous path to the tree. The steep cliff beneath me was slick with scree. Furious, I began to cut it, sawing at the wood. He woke with a scream. Black blood flowed from his ribs. I dropped the knife, bursting into tears. I felt like a worm crushed by the rain.

"Don't cry," he hushed me, comforting me through his pain.

"You're bleeding? But how?" I sobbed. Samael never bled.

"There is but one flower that grows in Hell," he hushed me, singing me to sleep as he once did. I hadn't understood at the time. His third eye opened while I slept, a blood-red jewel on his head. It pillaged my unformed brains, tilling the soil within. I had finally rebelled against him, and the season's cycle was nearing completion. The seed he carried needed a bearer. The soil was rich with potential. Later, I hoped he loved me for who I was, not what I would become for him. I always will, I suppose.

I was pure then, tabula rasa, a blank slate waiting for form. I knew I wasn't whole, and each day I moved further from Eden. What I searched for wasn't sleeping in the trees. It was hidden behind me, in his watchful gaze. I was a ghost before I'd met him. Haunting the hills as I lived on air. I would have been another discarded creation, save the potential he saw in me. I knew what I owed Samael. Like a rough diamond, Samael honed me into adamantine. The broken maker had seen past my flaws.

I came to think that was his power. To see the beauty in the most wretched of things. Nothing, god or angel, could see souls like Samael. But he was blind to his own reflection. He barely understood himself. I think it terrified him. He wore a skull to be spared of his eyes, then sought his reflection in drops of rain. After the night I hurt him, we entered a strange kind of peace. I stopped starving and maiming myself. He joined me in my firefly capture and would hunt them with quiet desperation. They were my playthings, like always.

If only I had known they were souls.

I grew taller and scaled trees to get the elusive jeweled bugs that crowned the canopy. Those were the souls of seraphim, like angels on Christmas Trees. He wove them into nets of pearls for my hair. I would dance for him as night fell, mimicking the flight of the butterfly. He would sing like the wind, sending me flying across the grass. I began to embrace my flesh, loved how it wrapped me in sensations. The touch of light and kiss of rain. I wondered if Samael could feel. I began to fear he felt nothing, and was just a dead tree that refused to fall.

When I was older, I understood our home was the place of death and dreams. Where he reigned, the twilight hours. I had been born into a graveyard. The ghosts I used to see began to fade. One morning, I woke unable to see the fireflies. My breasts were ripe and hips shapely like the wolves. The animals began to turn from me.

Even Samael changed. He began to move slower. His bones creaked. He spent more time sitting under his tree. He watched me, skull smiling as always. Sometimes, night and day would roll in, and he wouldn't move an inch. Dead leaves fell on his cloak, and I had to brush moss from his brow. I would kiss his cheek and sing to him. I pretended he was asleep.

Worms began to crawl through his skull. I plucked them from his eyes, begging him to wake up. "Please, Samael. Come run with me. I miss you, you know." I handed him an apple. It fell to the ground as his hands went limp. His teeth clattered as if he was trying to speak, but no voice came from within. He walked like a feeble man, leaning on my shoulder. We made it halfway down the hill until he collapsed. I carried his bones to the riverside and washed them in the water. Pests had eaten holes in them. I picked the bugs from his marrow.

The seasons turned. I became his guardian. I protected his bones from rot, washed him until my hands bled. It was months between his wakings. I hoped each time he would speak. His bones turned black, began to decay. The horror that I could truly be alone sat in my stomach like a stone. Whatever magic that had animated him finally left. I truly understood what death was. It wasn't an absence, but worse. It was him being ever there, but impossible to touch. It was a cruel lesson that he taught me.

One night, I took my knife. I skewered the obsidian into the tree. Hoping beyond hope he would wake. Pain had power, but it wasn't enough. The dead wood moaned; Samael's skull fractured. I cradled the broken pieces and cried.

Soon, the tree's branches fell. His bones had crumbled to dust. I kissed his remains, tasted death, and was driven out of Eden. In exile I walked, alone.

I wandered through the wastelands, Samael's cloak wrapped around me. It was a moth-eaten, molding thing, but the closest I had to a companion. Even the beasts of the fields would not come to me now. They sensed I was different. Human. It was why I'd grown deaf to their calls. I strayed to the sea, kept camp in a cave. I would sit for days like his skeleton, wishing that I could fade. I learned what Hell was then. It was being truly alone. I stopped eating, and delirium painted the shadows with him. I imagined Samael stood beside me, bowed as he asked for a dance. He took my hand and led me from the cave. We stood at the lip of the ocean. It felt like my heart, endless and lonely.

"Why did you leave me?" I asked him.

"I never left you, child. Now eat for me, please." He held me against his breast, stroked my hair, then danced into the evening fog. I swam into the sea after him, screaming after Samael. But he'd vanished. I cursed him, killed a fish and ate it raw. I grew strong to spite him. He was hideous, I decided. Unnatural and cruel. Even in death, he tormented me.

I left the beach and journeyed to the west, to the land where the sun died each night. It was lush and beautiful there, green beyond imagining. I tasted new fruits, learned how to survive in the different terrains. Samael's lessons served me well.

And then I met the man.

I knew that he was like me. Raised in the wild lands, alone in the world until then. We started a new life together, and what I thought was the golden age of my life faded to a pleasant dream. I all but forgot Samael and tucked him under the shadows of my dreams. My husband was of flesh and blood, and I took my place beside him. Some would come to call him Adamah, and say he gave me his rib. But my husband was not the first Adam, and it was not from his bones I was made. The first one abandoned me to the wasteland. It was necessary, I suppose, but how was I to know.

It was good, but the goodness didn't last. I loved Adam as I had learned to love Samael. I would sing and dance for him. We hunted and laughed together. Our conversations never ended, and we would spend blissful hours in each others' arms, exploring the second parts of our souls. He was so gentle and kind, like water in my hands. We felt like we were one, a being of clay, cleft in two, that fit perfectly back together.

But something in the heavens wanted us gone. Lightning would strike inches from our feet. The beasts grew a taste for man. Soft leaves I once rubbed my cheek against caused rashes to bloom on my skin. Nettles stung, thorns stuck, and sick meat poisoned us. One night wolves surrounded our camp, licking their hungry chops. I grabbed Adam's hand to run. Now I knew why Samael had chased me, so many moons ago. He was preparing me to be prey.

We moved north, to Samael's home. The hills of my childhood had changed. Everything was barren, frozen in perpetual winter. All the trees stood dead, and colorless shrubs dotted the dying grasses. Granite boulders had been exposed by the eroded soil. They stood sentinel over the valley that skirted Samael's tree. Walking past them was like being watched by inhuman gods. We eked out a living. It just grew colder and colder. I had no idea how to make clothes, possessed none of the arts of the angels. How could I? I didn't know they even existed. They had been watching us all this time, invisible. They'd driven Samael from his home and condemned his lands to Purgatory. The ice of the unliving beings left ghost trails of frost in the morning. His Tree, sleeping knowledge, had been changed to death. I would climb the hill when Adam was asleep and sit in its rotting boughs, sleeping under the freezing stars as I tried to remember the past. I prayed then, something I had no word for. I hoped the moon pitied me. All the things I never asked Samael bit at my heels like serpents. Had things really been so blissful that I never questioned my existence? I would have given anything for an hour with him.

The hope of some salvation faded. I knew, in my heart, we were dying. Adam didn't know what death was. I did. I wanted to protect him from it at all costs. Or maybe I just wanted to protect myself. He was like my youthful innocence, strong but so pure. He'd never washed someone's bones, nor imagined beetles could eat his flesh. We huddled in our cave, trying to share warmth. Each night, I walked the treacherous path to the tree. The ridges had crumbled away, and the spine of the trail nearly killed me. I left apples as desperate offerings, knowing they were pointless as I brought them nonetheless. The gentler fruits had died in the frosts, and only the hardy ones remained. Finally, the fruit went away. The game disappeared, we could catch no fish, so we survived on roots and bark.

I laid down one night and knew I would die. It was just a truth that appeared to me. I contemplated it for a while. Maybe I wanted to join Samael in the dust. The angels' presences did strange things to our minds. They twisted our thoughts and subdued us. But their spell was broken by his memory. The hill called to me, and I came.

The moon was achingly beautiful. I walked the path in anger, sick of sorrow and pain. If I was a bastard child, so be it.

I didn't recognize him that night. The wind bit at my bones. I heard the chains jangle and dogs howl in the wastelands. I should have known it was him. Instead, I saw a stranger.

All was still. I walked slowly towards him. He stood at the base of the tree. I saw him and thought I had died.

The branches grew from his ribs. The stranger was beautiful and bone pale, dressed in severe black robes. He smiled, somber, almost mad. He was everything I tried to touch in the flames. I thought that he would burn me.

He beckoned me to come closer. I flew like a moth to his light, standing a mere foot from him. His eyes were the clear blue of desert pools. I wanted to run to his arms.

"Samael?" I asked, not believing it. I thought him a delusion of my mind.

"Do not be afraid," he whispered.

"I'm dying, Samael."

"I know." He hushed me as I sobbed into his breast. I cried out in wonder and sorrow. He was so beautiful, but I had only this moment with him. I had lived my life with his shadow, always carried his bones. He kissed me, soothed me as he never could before. I didn't care if he was my imagining. His voice coiled with life; the arms that held me were like my own. Not the whisper of graves or touch of dry bone. Even Adam could not complete me like this. I wondered if he had been Samael's creation, to keep me from being alone.

I burrowed my head against his chest, waiting to die. His heart beat in tandem with my failing one. I understood my nakedness before him, the low creature that I was. Midnight came to Eden. He pressed his hand into the small of my back, like he wanted to slip under my skin. I ended where he began, circle dancing in his heart. He wiped the tears from my eyes and whispered into my hair.

"You are my flower, Eve." He drew the hem of his robe back, exposing his chest. I kissed the white flesh, finally able to touch his life. My tears caught like dew on his skin. I couldn't speak, silenced by his magnificence. He was like the moon I prayed to.

He sliced a crescent across his chest. Samael peeled back his flesh, broke away the ribs. They were bone branches, parts of the Tree. Death's heart pulsed before me. I was horrified. It beat like infinity. He revealed the essence of his divinity, all the knowledge I sought. It lived before me, under his skin. I was so removed from the moment, contemplating the angel's beauty, that I didn't realize the gravity of his act.

Humans walked bare through earth. Angels cloaked themselves. Seraphim hid behind wings. Samael had masked himself in my childhood. But now, Death bared his soul. The greatest taboo of all. He revealed himself to a mortal and broke the barrier between us. If only I had known what that would mean.

"I have only one heart to give."

He reached into himself, gaze calm and cold like an arctic sea. Amusement, pain, and intensity flickered across his eyes. Once more, his face was cryptic. I will never know what he thought. He took his heart. Gave it to me. He was the only warmth in the bleakness of Eden. A place of absolute zero, soon to be devoid of life.

"Partake of my flesh. Eat."

"I can't," I protested, revolted.

"Take it, Havah. It's yours."

There was no fruit on the dead tree. I held the only bloom of winter.

I cradled it in my hands. Pressed it to my lips. His fire entered me. I screamed out, insides burning. But it was such a beautiful pain. He cradled me in his arms as I was truly brought to life.

My maker was left with a black hole for a heart. A pit that devours and consumes. Lust for the life that was once his. Death and I were born.

"I will always love you, girl."

Everything changed that day. I passed it on to Adam. Death entered our veins. My protector in Eden banished me from our home. He kept my heart with him. Such was the price of freedom.

The original sin was love. Its coals are coals of fire. Stronger than death and the grave. The very flames of my lord.

Winter came to Eden. Oh, how it left us bare.

For now, I wait
til spring.

THE GIRL WHO COULD NOT FLY

Once upon a time, God grew lonely in Heaven. This was back in the days when everything was lush and green, not a flower out of place in Paradise or fruit tainted by winter frost. Despite all its beauty and his beloved sons, he yearned for a companion, and so he made a girl without wings. He thought to keep her only to himself. Even God was young in those days. He named himself Adam, called her Eve, and everything was good for a time.

Each day, she would watch the birds and sigh, wishing like her brothers, she had wings. All Eve wanted, she could not reach. God granted her every wish, but still, she yearned for more.

"Adam," she said. "As a child, I fell in love with the stars. If only you could give me the sun."

Adam laughed. "But Eve, our place is the ground, dreaming of what lies above. It is the way of the world."

She did not hear him. "If only you could lend me a pair of the angels' wings. I would but for a moment know peace."

God sighed, relented, and pressed them onto her shoulders, formed from the aether and clouds.

"Do not venture too close, sister, otherwise, the sun shall destroy you," Adam warned. For the sun was voracious, and cared little who he burned.

"Yes God," she said, but like moths to a flame, flew too close. They say Eve's fall was like the Morning Star. "Oh Sun!" she cried. "Wed me!" But the sun is an unthinking thing. It laughed and cast her down, a bruised and broken girl. As she fell, he smiled.

"What are you?" Eve howled. "Who?"

He echoed her call like a bird. "Who? Who are you?"

"I am Eve."

"I am what I am."

She contemplated this as she fell. He struck her with his light and impregnated her.

In the cadence, Eve gave birth to the moon. Women and the children of stars never got along well.

God caught her on impact. She cried as he gave her a bath. From the tarry suds rose a kill of crows. Eve was dying, so he took his heart and placed it in her breast, then donned the blackened wings as his own. Furious, he cast her out.

"You have cursed us all," he cried. "Now, I hath become death, winter will come to the garden, and we will know lives of toil."

But Eve smiled, for she knew the truth- after all, she had seen the black heart of a star.

"You are eternal, oh God. You are all that is."

He was too far gone to reply.

HOW DEATH FELL IN LOVE WITH THE MOON

Before the time of the angels, when God was truly alone, a gardener of a gestating world, Death came into being.

Samael, as he came to be known, was bones before God invented flesh, bare white with a perpetual grin.

His Father looked out one thorny morning through Eden's vines upon the falling snow. He noted the blankness and thought, in His wisdom, "It is good. I shall create in My image one who walks with winter and brings about the harvest of souls." And so, out of frost and slices of star, God fashioned Death, the master of souls.

Death was a creation of night, eye hollows holding captive the abyss from which the Lord had arose. God loved his son Death for his terribleness, but pitied him for his soft heart. For Death, in his innocence, thirsted for life, not knowing he was the end of it.

"My Father, what is my name?" Death asked, examining his bony hands. "For what have you created me? I feel a terrible pain."

God smiled, looking upon his confused son. "Every creature must discover their own truths," He said, voice like a lion. "In them, you shall find your name, and the purpose for your creation. Go, child, out into the world. As for the pain: birth hurts, son, and life is harder still, but you will find ways to clothe yourself. The pain is meant to protect you. It is my ultimate gift."

And with that God dismissed him, casting him into the wilderness. Death wandered aimlessly for minutes or years, until the seasons changed thrice and thrice again. (Time was a fickle thing in Eden, ill-formed and looped like a labyrinth.) Death loved the blossoming honeysuckle, the blooms of jasmine and rose. Yet whenever he plucked them, they withered in his hand. His footsteps left ash in their wake.

Death was walking barrenness, naked, and sorrowed at the destruction he left. One desperate day, watching a silkworm weave its cocoon, he was struck by inspiration. "If I could but weave as the silkworm does, I would surely not kill the flowers I love." Snatching his shadow from the ground, Death fashioned a black robe that slipped over him like a glove, covering him in silky darkness. He too now had a cocoon, and his touch did not kill. But still, he found, he was pained. Now that flowers did not wither in his grasp, he found he longed for life even more.

It was a biting need Death had, a hunger, and Death found himself rabid with appetite. He tried to sate it with fruits and tubers, but nothing filled his hollow soul.

The full moon hung high above him, sleeping, and Death, desperate, plucked her from the sky, delicately eating her as though she were a juicy globe. Not wanting to destroy her entirely, for Death found her beautiful, he placed her back in the sky, now cratered from Death's bite.

The moon awoke and cried out "You have wounded me!" She turned her back to Death, refusing to shine light upon him. Death stumbled about in the darkness, glowing with her light. Death's hunger ceased, replaced by a horrible burning, and he realized what he had done. The moon, God's mirror, reflected God's glorious heart. In devouring her, he had taken into himself bits of Creation. Death thrummed with life, a gift God had denied him, and in blazes of pain flesh began to form a prison round Death's bones. He roared with the agony, awakening God, who rushed to Death's side.

The moon informed God what Death had done, and God simply laughed, watching over his foolish son. "So you have tasted fruit from the Tree of Life, child," God said. "I suppose I never forbade you. You will wax and wane as the moon now, alive and not alive, just a reflection of life, shining dead light into this world. The moon will be your crescent blade, and her tides will pull on your soul."

Death looked down upon his new form, at the strong hands and pale skin, and found them beautiful. He saw his face in God's ineffable eyes: hair that hung long and black as night, irises like pools of sky, a mouth cruel as a hawk's. He could hardly imagine himself plucking roses now. The hunger, sated for only a moment, sprung to life again with a vengeance. Now that Death had tasted life, he desired it even more. He realized for what he had been created.

"You made me to destroy," Death said, in shock, touching the harsh lines of his cheekbones.

God chuckled. "Is that the truth you have found?"

Death hung his head. "I should have realized it before this. I am no gardener like you. No tender of blooms or fields. I serve as your reaper, Father. And I think you cruel, to have created me so."

God's humor faded. He looked at His son with concern. "It was with love I brought you into this world, child. And it is with love that you should serve. Do not hate what you are."

"How can I not? I am poison. Sama'el, the Venom of God. I blacken all I touch."

"No. You are Sama'el, the Drug of the Lord. Drugs, in the right dosage, can be medicine, can heal. It is your choice how you wield your powers: to purify or bring ruin."

Samael fled from the Lord, convinced he was cursed by his Father. His hunger gnawed at him with the strength of Abaddon, the Pit. The time of the angels came and went, the time of man dawned, and Samael waxed into life with the full moon and waned into death with her darkness. Much happened in between, as things are wont to do, and Samael found himself in the thick of it all, ever tied to the Tree of Life, first thief of her fruit- for the fruit of that Tree is souls.

But those stories are for another time, and this tale is only a half-truth, a lie formed in the bed of ruin. All I know is that Death watches the moon, tears in his crystalline eyes, singing a song that would break the world. When I ask why he is sorrowed, he is silent, and the pain on his face could fill the book of life. A thousands scribes could not record it, poets could not capture the suffering, and artists would spend a lifetime trying to sketch his grief. His song is an old one, in some dead language that perhaps not even the angels remember, if it is even a language at all.

Only the moon knows why he weeps. Were that I were her.

FALL FROM HEAVEN. FALL LIKE HELL.

Lucifer is lost, they say, he wandered astray at the fork between the Milky Way and the Perseid's, hitched a ride on a comet with his manifold silver white wings and landed in darkness, far from the light of the furthest star. His halo of golden hair glowed like a jellyfish in the depths of deep space, bioluminescent divinity oozing out of flaming keratin like a song heard by no one, for in the outer rim, there is no sound.

Just silence.

Lucifer's compass broke – don't you know men that are birds and birds that are men have magnetic bits in their skull like geese and migrate always North? The Fall scrambled the pieces of lodestone etched in Lucifer's skull and now, he wanders the wastes that have become Pandemonium over time, fractals of fallen angels finding a lightless abode in the void and populating it with lost dreams.

They say if Lucifer could fix the broken map of his mind, he would come roaring back into Heaven and accuse Michael. He would lay every mishap caused by the Angel of the Lord at the Prince of Heaven's feet and throw vitriolic acid that would turn leaden pinions to gold, coal to diamonds, and rain to splinters of ice.

Lucifer would sob into Michael's arms, ranting and raving, clutching at the broken ribs of his damnation like a madman as they poked through his papery skin and say, "Brother, look what I have become, this wasted thing. Why did you let me go? Why did you cast me out? We could have reigned together."

And Michael would run his scarred fingers through the cornsilk of his older twin's hair and warmed his Kelvin zero demon with the mercy of God. "Because, brother, I had to let you know God, and the only way you seem capable of comprehending the love of the Lord is by shunning it, running from the very thing that gave you life, and then mourning the loss of Someone that would welcome you back into His arms without a word. You were the one who cast us out, Morning Star."

And Lucifer would bite his lip, and he and Michael would share a bitter kiss, like day old coffee grounds and the rind of an unripe pear, and that would be the end and beginning of Lucifer's questions.

Silence.

SERPENT-TOOTH

"Stop your bitching. It's business, Samael. Pure,
sheer work of G-d. We're men of the book, after
all."

"You kill her, and I'll scythe your butt-buddy Gabe to shiny little bits."

Michael said nothing, gaze stony. Samael hesitated, drawing a quick breath.

"Now Michael, I know we've had our falling outs in the past. But I have a little offer that might just interest you."

Silence. His golden lips open, voice like thunder.

"I'm listening."

"We're men of the world, brother. We know what's coming. Let's say, theoretically, that we cast our lots together. "

"A radical proposition."

"Radical times, the world in flames- Michael, we've been here before. But let's say we feed this fire together, or together, put it out, instead of incessantly thwarting each other. Damn equilibrium to hell! Let chaos reign. There would be many benefits to reap from it."

"Once more, you care nothing for others, brother. I am justice, law. You are wickedness, selfish desire, and blind as the cratered moon."

"I am judgement, Michael. Do not forget that."

"Is that so, Samael? You still delude yourself that you are holy, worthy of redemption?" Michael smiled- not a true smile, never true- but a cold tilt of the lips completely devoid of warmth. "You have nothing in your heart. I ripped it from you. How could you possibly love? You do not love; you comprehend nothing. Your truths are twisted lies."

Michael moved closer, like a lion towards a snake. "Without a heart, your words mean nothing. I will never stand with you."

Samael narrowed his eyes, fire flashing in their unfathomable depths.

"It was never my heart to begin with," he whispered, voice like nails under stone.

For the first time in centuries, Michael's face shadowed with emotion. The fading whisper of...

"What?" he said, voice like cracking ice.

Samael smirked, dark laughter rising from the bowels of his throat. "Kill the girl, Michael. Kill her, and you lose all you have fought for."

"Spit it out, Samael."

"Why should I? I have nothing to gain by telling you. You will not play along with me, brother. So be it. But fate- it is tied by blood. Is that not right, Lightbearer?"

Michael pinned Samael with his glacial gaze. The depths of Sheol stared back.

"I am nothing like you, Samael."

"Not yet, brother. I am the darker reflection. But mirrors can be reversed. Our wickedest fears come true."

"Pity the day they do," Michael said, almost mocking.

Samael sneered. "Gravity is undeniable, brother- and even the brightest apples fall..."

THE TEMPTATION OF ASMODEUS

Raphael's manacles on my wrists burned me, sinking me like a stone into the foul water where seabirds and fish schooled in wretched pools around me.

"No!" I cried. "Sarai? SARAI!"

"Repent, foul demon," the peerless, blazing archangel said, scalding my ram horns off at their base with his fiery pendulum of a blade. It glowed even brighter than Uriel's damned inferno rapier. "The world shall not miss you."

I thought of Sarai, soft. Her hips under my lips. How she cried to me when Tobias stole into her tent and raped her. How she had trembled in my arms each time I, Ashmedai, had gutted one of the foul rotten thieves, hangmen, and abusive pieces of dogshit her father Raguel, the damn doddering bastard, had tried to sell her off to for money.

The stone I was chained to sunk, more boulder than pillar, carved with the Shem HaMephorash. The angelic Names blazed with G-dly fire and the disgusting, pure and hellish water poisoned my flesh like the cantarella Sarai had once pressed into my lips on our stolen wedding night, under the fig she had planted long ago. I screamed her name, but bubbles and a sweltering whirlpool worthy of Scylla swallowed

me, Ashmedai

whole.

First, the wings went. Then the lion, dragon, and man heads, reduced to skull. My bowlegged chicken feet stayed longest, true shedim style, but these blasted fish, they are hungry.

Bones last millennia, you know.

Revile, revulsion, revelation. I had many times of sun's revolution under that Sea of Galilee. Then, a sudden storm. Some great white feet, far leagues above, walking on water? Impossible. A heavenly glow – like Raphael – but kinder.

A voice that spoke.

"Come to me, my child," like a rough fisherman's.

Hands, they reached. Pulled me up into a boat.

A Jewish man, hundreds of years later, with the peerless mark of G-d.

"You are no man, to pull devils from the water," I said, a bestial archdemon skeleton.

"I am unlike no Son of Man you have ever met before, dear Ashmedai. Tell me, do you regret Sarai?"

The man had a close crop of dark hair, olive eyes, and tan, roughshod skin – hands scarred and callused, like he worked hard with them. He smelled like spring water.

"Regret her?" My voice was rough, unused. I had been with my thoughts for mayhaps a thousand years. "No. I never forgot her brown eyes. Her beautiful, hooded nose. The elegant plumes of her plump, kind flesh. Her rebellion. I will not follow you, Son of G-d. I am not meant for the angels."

"Ashmedai, thine too are a Son of G-d." With that, the strange man touched me, and restored me to the human form I had so often taken to visit Sarai bat Raguel. "She is waiting for you in a glade in Gan Eden, Ashmedai, son of David and Agrath bat Mahalath."

I flexed my hands, crying. Fine black talon, supple black curls, deep black eyes, olive deep proud scarred skin, nothing that would scare her.

"But... she is dead. Gone to Hades. Or Heaven, with that blasted Tobias or Raphael. I do not know, Sir–?"

"Yeshua."

"That is a strange name. You are holy. As if – as if G-d. But no. Nothing is sowed of a virgin unseeded."

Yeshua gave a strange smile, his dark olive eyes dancing. "Would you like to believe a little, in Him and me, Ashmedai, humble fisherman and servant of my Father I may simply be? A fisherman on Galilee knows tricks. There are monsters in these waters, Ashmedai."

I shivered, suddenly frightened by his holiness. I saw him with my foreknowledge at the End, Sword at His Hand, Sparing None of My Kind.

But, no. He would do better than Father. He was my brother, I knew it!

"You are from David's line. You are more talented than Solomon."

Yeshua smiled trick-sweet, touching my brow.

Horns sprouted from them again, my Covenant with G-d, like Moshe of old.

"Fly to her on your wings, Ashmedai, up the Jacob's Ladder to the North of Kesil the Hangman. I have opened Dumah's gate for you," Yeshua said, pulling up his fishing net, walking back onto the water with those blazing white feet, and leaving me bobbing quite in shock in that plain fisherman boat that smelled of salt.

I summoned my wings, dumbstruck. But I smelled... jasmine. Oud. A must that was her.

Sarai.

The stars birthed electricity, and I felt Sarai's call. I knew, souls are immortal, and there was no punishing angel that could ever condemn me to a world without my Daughter of Raguel, trickster like this Yeshua she was.

So I flew, up to Heaven.

Sarai was there, her breasts heavy in a pomegranate black glass bead dress like the Egyptians used to make. She held an ewer of water to a trough of heavenly goats, a humble ramshackle hut in Gan Eden – clearly alone. No Tobias or Raphael in sight. My mother Bathsheba was cooking in the kitchen, Abigail was hanging laundry to dry, and David and Solomon were chopping wood for a fire. Even Absalom and Tamar worked dying fabric.

"What is this place, my bashert?" I asked, falling to my knees, weeping in my Sarai's lap.

Sarai laughed. "So you met Him. G-d offered me a choice too, my Ashling. Now, I too am a Daughter of David. Welcome home to your palace – now cottage – my love."

And now, Bathsheba combs my hair like she used too, Abigail critiques the way I herd the flock, always happy I am too busy making love to Sarai to not lose a stray lamb – not that Abigail would ever admit she

didn't mind me neglecting my diligence for my wife
– and David, Solomon and I fly kites in the evening,
out of paper from China, in the shape of mine own
dragon wings.

G-d forgives all, and in G-d, all is remade.

Even I, Ashmedai, Lover of Women, Husband of A
Woman, Servant of G-d, Father of

Little Shoshanna and Jeremiah.

"I never forgot you," Sarai and I say each night,
and that

Is all

Ashmedai needs.

TO REIGN IN HELL

In Hell, in the beginning, there was darkness, like God put out the moon with his thumb.
Satan fell, and his tears froze the lowest circle. Satan's love is a burning thing, but his agony is absolute cold.

Beelzebub was the first to fall. The first to carry the banner and sound the horn for the Mourning Star. He was the first to bleed, the first to storm Heaven's Gates. Satan's wise counselor, most trusted general, and above all, esteemed companion.

They are alone together for what seems like eternity, Beelzebub with his insect wings torn by the incinerating atmosphere, Satan plucking his mangled feathers dry as he goes mad, not even noticing he is freezing. Beelzebub's king is singing a song Father used to sonorously paint their cradles with. Satan makes it sweet and wretchedly cruel:

My sons, my darling shining stars.

Smolder bright like embers from afar.

But up close, sons, burn them to flames.

Thy Kingdom Come, all worlds to claim.

For each word, a broken bit of white down.

For each verse, an infidel kingdom crushed for Christendom.

For each syllable, a dead god, a cold idol, a coffin for the false spirits.

Satan repeats it over and over, his tears blue banners.

Beelzebub waits. Finally, there is light, after perhaps the trillionth repetition.

A third of Heaven falls as stars of simmering bright flesh, a flash of brilliance.

Then impact on jagged rocks and ice. Reformation and mutation into monsters.

Pain.

They build an empire on ash and bone, and bury the brothers and sisters that do not survive the Fall. In honor, much later, when some semblance of civilization is build, however twisted, they put their gravestones into the mortar of the Capital's building.

Pain, memories, wine like blood, or is it blood like wine?

There is not much to say at night, but it is always night in Hell.

Beelzebub remembers, Satan grows more wicked, so far from his former brightness, and falls into madness and depravity.

Beelzebub holds the kingdom together, runs martial drills for the War That Never Ends.

Beelzebub goes over the ledgers and public records, holds councils, takes too short nights of comfort in his sweet boys.

Usually, he is alone in his tower.

Better to reign in Hell than serve in Heaven?

Only if Heaven was ever perfect in the first place.

The Lord of Flies looks up at the stars of dead god's hearts, stitched into the fabric of the void. You see, the demons had to improvise. All that were left were corpses after the conquest, and after all, all souls eventually end up here.

I sit with Bael, Baal Zebub, a memory of Baal Hadad, or maybe he has always been a spider.

We entwine in his web and kiss venom and poison and toxins.

There are jewels in his web, lost treasures of a thousand conquered kingdoms.

Maggots eat Satan's corpse, flies emerge from the dregs of the Grim Reaper. Satan's true name is Samael, after all – the finality of the scythe, and before his scythe, his spear.

Beelzebub would eat his shit if it purified his brother. He has drank Satan's tears, swallowed his cum, bathed in his blood, all to feel again.

It is a cold night in Hell.

Beelzebub looks up at the stars.

There is mist in his eyes.

Tear for every dead brother.

A sob for a negligent parent.

I miss my Father, Chava. Sometimes, it takes all I have to just go on.

I take his bone white hand – my albino angel, or my red-eyed demon with platinum hair, black capes, and gauntlets.

I speak without thought:

You have our brethren's love. Asmodeus. Samael. Rofocale. Belial. Lilith. Asherah. From the Archdemons to the Goetics to the lowliest Damned. You have us.

He gives a ghost of a smile.

Yes, you, our angel in Hell. Sometimes, Chava, you are the only light here. I am the Lord of Creeping Things, of the soft rabbits and soft souls, the moths and butterflies, your soul is a doe or a hare. I am frost, ice, and fire – Hell is primal, fire and water, but I shall keep you warm. In Hell, the only light is love.

Never lose your kindness, Chava. It is innocence
demons cherish above all.
Baal Hadad rides the storm, be they frost or fire.
Some gods died in those ancient celestial wars.
Some took on different names.
Some forgot their own holiness.
For all of them, Beelzebub remembers.

GENESIS REMIXED

When Chavah awoke in the Garden, she was filled with regret. What was once rib, now flesh, did not feel whole. Her husband slept as G-d led her, an automaton given Breath and Word, through Gan Eden.

Shortly after Adam first forced her to submit, on the hard red clay he was made from, Chavah's cries summoned a beautiful siren with raven hair and emerald bezels in her eyes. The maven rode a cherry red Harley, this Lilith, and had an extra pink helmet with daisies she had drawn in chalk paint on it for Chavah.

Chavah was quite impressed by Lilith's nose ring, generous hips and breasts, and tattoos like a barista on the lam.

Having just been made that morning, Chavah had nothing to pack. All Chavah knew was that her destiny lay with this dazzling serpent woman, in her leather jacket, smoking Virginia Slims. They were meant to cleave, be helped and helpmate, master and servant, mistress and lover and laughter, and create beauty.

So, Chavah put on a red checkered sundress, wedged heels (out of fashion sense, of course - not covered out of shame of nakedness. Bareness is for rudimentary creations like Adam, but Liliths and Chavahs like to accessorize) and saddled Lilith's Harley, the sun skipping over their luscious locks as they sped, hellbent, out of Gan Eden, and into the wide green world.

First, they traversed the universe, making camp at night under Adonai's cosmos, and angels and demons alike attended them with food, manna, and figs. Chavah kept a sketchbook, a stenciled Moleskin, where she did figure studies of her wife, and botanical drawings. Lilith liked to carve seashells and coral into jewelry to adorn Chavah.

Lilith taught Chavah secrets – Adonai's name, how a pearl was formed on an oyster's tongue, and a diamond forged out of carbon deep in the depths of the Earth. But Chavah taught Lilith pleasure in a way that distant Sammael never had – where men fail, women understand.

They cast stars upon each other's bodies and drank down mountain dew and honey wild from their chalices. When they made love, even Dumah, angel of silence, was known to weep.

Those were the days of great making. The universes coalesced, coiled, spiraled out like the Shekinah's hair, and the Shekinah shone brightly down on her handmaiden, Lilith, and her chosen daughter, Chavah.

They walked in the light of Adonai, crafting fantasies and terpsichores from the spindrifts of cavemen dreams. Adam had multiplied with his second nameless wife, the one who G-d constructed before Adam's very eyes, flesh upon muscle upon bone, and soon, Chavah and Lilith were relegated to the realm of myths.

The People cried out: give us succor, Asherah. So, Lilith and Chavah became a Tree, menorah-shaped, and grew fruit to feed their sons and daughters. Only Adam, immortal, hacked the Shekinah Tree of Knowledge down. In revenge, Lilith planted a vine – grapes that she and Chavah taught their daughters to make wine so splendid, it inspired poetry and deeds of greatness in men of valor and the daughters of the Watchers.

A flood came. A great one. Towers were built and toppled. First, clay cities, then wood, then stone, then the bones of earth raped to form great metal beams and skyscrapers. Moloch of industry arose, consuming dreams. Mammon created empires fat off his coffers. Ashmedai seduced. Beelzebub possessed. Sammael was set against Michael at every turn.

But Chavah and Lilith? They infused the world with beauty. Feminism. Revolution. Science and the Renaissance. Democracy. For every mother kissing her child, there was Chavah. For every blue stockinged lass carving her way in a man's world, there was Lilith.

Eventually, they opened a bakery. Challah was their specialty, with seven twisted braids. They kept bees out back, the wives Lilith and Chavah, and they read Tarot and the threads of fate for the young maidens and boys who came to them for advice. For widows and those who lost a child – whether to Dumah or abortion or infertility – they gave free coffee, fresh honeycomb, and bread.

It was a man's world, but slowly, gently, women reigned. We, their daughters, created peace, endless beauty and succor, so no son died in war, and every daughter was cradled and wanted. Lilith and Chavah continued serving the Shekinah, and the women of the world finally tasted the Fruit of Life.

Southern Simmers

It was born of two women, first and last, alpha and omega, snake and snake charmer.

And now, Lilith and Chavah live in our hearts, and if you seek out to find them, bread and cheese in hand at midnight, through Alice's looking glass, you will come to their café, and the Mothers of Life and Death will braid your curls free of sorrow.

And all that starts well, ends well. They will wipe your tears, kiss your cheeks, make you a mocha, flat white, or comforting latte, and the fire in your heart to carry on will be kindled, and the Foundresses of Humanity will sing you into this life and the next, carry you to the far shores of wonder, miracles, and the wild, and on their motorcycle, you'll ride.

SATAN DISCOVERS THE INTERNET (AND STARTS A 2010'S WORDPRESS BLOG)

To my hideous chagrin, the Worm's taken it upon herself to discover what I am:

Worm, also known as "Eve": "So you're not a demon, Sam? You're like a double-timing angel? A maverick? Like Sarah Palin?-"

Me: "Don't compare me to that Alaskan filth, maggot."

Worm: "But your Wikipedia page says you're "equitable with Satan and the chief of evil spirits." That sounds like Palin to me."

Me: "My Wikipedia page is written by ignorant louses that've never have a religious experience in their pitiful lives. I'm Death , you dimwit- most mortals won't meet me until they die, yet they insist on making up all these idiot opinions about me on the basis of prejudice alone. It's propaganda. Just look at this! " Samael is one of the seven regents of the world and is served by two million angels ." That's not even half of the amount of girls I keep as concubines."

Worm: (Horrified) "Please tell me you're joking."

Me: (Smirk) "Perhaps. But you believed me for a moment there, didn't you. Stop looking at this trash and go to the library- I know it's a revolutionary concept. Your generation demands instant gratification via technology. Did you know information was once won through a hard-fought battle of research ? Scholars poured through vellum texts in dank monasteries, committed logarithmic tables to memory before the invention of the calculator, sat with their abaci under the burning Greek sun-"

Worm: "Hah! You sound like an old fogey. Get with the times, Grimmy. You haven't even learned how to drive yet."

Me: "I can too drive, you sliming annelid."

Just look at my hot rod. And that's not the only thing in this picture I'd ride...

Worm: "Just not well. Fine, I'll go to the library, if you insist."

So she proceeded to go to the library. Instead of searching the catalogues like any sensible woman, or going to the religion or folklore departments, she went to the fiction shelves.

Me: "Why'd you go to the bloody novel section? What do you think I am, fictional ?"

Worm: "You are ."

Me: "So should I plunge my 'fictional' scythe into your pulsing jugular, eh?"

Worm: "No! I just mean that most people think you're unreal. So- So I went and tried to find something on angels-"

Me: "This- (brandishing book) is not scholarly research. It's a bloody story."

Worm: "It's called Angelology ! And you're in the d@mn thing! You said your other name was Sam-Yah-Zah, right? (grumbling) Look- you're even on the dumb cover..."

Me: (hurls book to the floor, voice venomous) " No , you sniveling, raisin-brained plebe: that's a starved clone of Bon Jovi melodramatically brooding in the shadows-"

Worm: "READ THE BOOK."

Me: "I've already absorbed it's contents, fool. I don't need to read it like a common mortal. All the Watchers in it look like an army of David Bowies.

What the bleeding Gehenna is that ? I'd rather stick a pike up my @ss than be blond ."

Worm: "Hey! I like my hair, and so do guys-"

Me: "Because it lowers your IQ by 20 points. Your hair is the color of piss."

Worm: (near tears) "I hate you! You're ruining my life! I can't even have my friends over anymore because you refuse to leave! You don't even put the d@mn lid down on the toilet. Why the heck do you even need to pee?"

Me: "I don't, actually. I just do it to spite you."

Worm: " Wow . You really are Satan."

Me: "At your service, my dear."

Worm: "So you are the devil?"

Me: "I never said that. Satan just means "Adversary," it's a title that many others have. I'm the adversary of mankind- I present your sins before you upon your death, then judge you accordingly. If I find your soul pure, I allow you to pass on to Heaven or Nirvana or Asgard or where-ever-the-hell you want to go. And if not, well... (smiles darkly) You'll see when you die."

Worm: "I seriously hope you've retired by then."

Me: "Fat chance, Worm. Actually, Chance is a skinny bitch- What the hell is this ? (Picks up paper I found tucked under books on the table)"

Worm: (snickering) "What Angelology's cover should really look like."

Me: "What- this is me ? This isn't funny, you brat! And what the bleeding heck am I sitting on?"

Worm: "A mausoleum. It's your death-bed."

Me: "... And I suppose I'm wearing a shroud ?"

Worm: (cackling with laughter)

Me: "You are a sick, depraved individual."

Worm: "Wait, what are you doing? Don't burn it ! It was just a joke!"

Me: "Try and stop me, maggot!- Get that fire extinguisher out of my face , you impertinent wretch!"

So upon threat of being sprayed, I left the bloody drawing alone. I'm beginning to think my host, though dumb, is also seriously disturbed. Who in their right mind would deliberately mock Death ? Perhaps she's suicidal.

...

Or just a dumb blonde.

So the Worm decided to make an omelet today. Of course, the idiot doesn't know how to cook, so she went prancing about the kitchen like a fool, grabbing spices and hurling them into the mixture without thinking twice. Why the hell she lobbed in bunches of Cajun Spices, Old Bay Seasoning, Red Pepper, and a sh*tload of garlic powder is beyond me. When I warned her she might not live to see evening, she shrugged and dumped the mess into the frying pan, letting it burn and dissolve into a cheese-covered-black-and-yellow monstrosity. It stank worse than brimstone. Then, of course, she ate the d@mn thing . There was a foul smelling garlic-and-pepper cloud that clung to her all afternoon- I had to leave the pathetic excuse for a house to avoid gagging on the stench.

She's now moaning in her room, close to puking her guts out.

This morning just serves to remind me of why I love idiots . They're amusing beyond belief. Humans were only created to entertain the deities, anyways. I mean, what use could a species that deliberately gives itself food poisoning be? The eggs weren't even cooked all the way- there's probably legions of salmonella bacteria having an asexual orgy in her gut. I give her a 50/50 chance at survival.

Now, I'm not a misanthrope- I swear on your undug grave. But in my line of work, you come to realize just how ridiculous humans are. They die in the most hilarious ways. Jonestown massacre ? Please. That was natural selection. Did you know that in 1000 AD, many communities throughout Europe literally thought it was going to be the End of the World ? So they partied like it was the Apocalypse, consuming all their stores of food for the winter in massive End of Days feasts, then locked themselves up in the town church on December 31, expecting to be Raptured come morning.

Much to their shock, the townspeople woke to find that, GASP, nothing had happened.

They then promptly starved to death.

Ironic, right? Oh, don't look at me like I'm a depraved, twisted b@stard. It was their own bloody faults. Just like the Worm. She might die because she insisted on eating an omelet that the Angel of bloody DEATH told her not to.

Humans do stupid things.

I'm sufficiently less drunk today, for the first time in a week. And without the perpetual alcoholic haze clouding my vision, I've come to realize something:

Mortals creep the f*ck out of me.

As you might have gathered, I'm currently crashing with a mortal. On pain of death, of course- she doesn't have much choice in the matter. She's also one of the few humans in the area who wouldn't try to exorcise me or think I'm after their soul if I suddenly took up residence in their abode.

Why, you ask? Because she's an idiot. She's utterly useless to me, anyways, so I suppose she thinks she's safe. How this ridiculous notion entered her head, I haven't a clue. I suppose she has an unconscious death wish- those are always so tempting to exploit. And I rarely ever resist temptation, so here I am, exploiting it.

But my host seems to have disturbing tendencies. Just this morning, I was sitting at her pathetic excuse of a table, drinking coffee I'd forced her to brew me, and I found this:

The depraved little wretch has drawn a picture of me. After nearly blasting off her head with a string of chthonic curses and criticizing her for her pathetic attempt at art, I demanded she explain why she sh@t out this little piece of sin from the rotting stew of her brain:

Worm (or host, I suppose): (Shrugs) "I dunno. I was bored, and you stole my computer again, so I had nothing better to do. Did you know that when you're mad, smoke literally comes out of your head? Something on the Internet must've really pissed you off. You set off my frigging smoke alarm."

Me: (gives Worm the Glare of Death) "I was reading more idiotic, mortal drool about "angelic

69

experiences." Bring me your laptop, wretch." (Shows Worm website)

Worm: (reading website aloud) "'Have you ever felt like you were being watched?'... By what, Peeping Toms? Government agents? ' No, not like in a bad way. More like a loving way.' Oh God- she's one of those Touched by an Angel fanatics!"

Me: (scoffs) "Exactly. The only kind of watching I do-"

Worm: (glares) "I know, you psychotic b@stard! Stay out of the frigging bathroom when I take a shower! I put the fracking locks on! How did you even get in, you perv?" (She would have pummeled me at this point, if she hadn't known I was infinitely stronger than her and she didn't stand a chance)

Me: (snickers) "No door stops Death. And I'm a Watcher. My eyes can see everything, worm. Just be glad I'm not Azazel, otherwise I'd be liable to act on my impulses."

Worm: (utterly confused) "Eh? Who the heck is Uh-Zay-Zul? And what do you mean act on your impulses? You have no self-restraint! I'm sick of coming home from work and finding you sprawled across my bed naked with random chicks from the bar! Stop creeping on me when I'm changing, and GET OUT OF MY HOUSE!"

Me: (summons scythe)

Worm: "..... I mean, um, do whatever you want! A-heh-heh... Get that thing away from me! I'm too young to die!"

Me: "You're ripe for the plucking, whelp. Now get. You're giving me a bloody migraine. And IF I find you making these hideous drawings again, it's off with your head !"

Worm: (runs screaming out of the room) "AAAAGH!"

Me: "Argh, my head!" (winces at migraine, glances at picture) "Freaky b*tch... the proportions on this thing burn my eyes...!"

Hideous, isn't it? Not only do I look constipated, I also have womanly hands. I couldn't do this job with those sticks as fingers. Does she think hauling this scythe is easy? Those are the hands of wretched, brooding artistic types that make me vomit up lava.

Now you're probably wondering about demonic physiology. Don't. It's too complicated for your numb little mind to comprehend.

But I'd like to make something clear: I'm not Lucifer. Well, not really. We're often confused for one another, though we do share many qualities . The comic of Neil Gay-man uses "Samael" as the angelic name of Lucifer, which is incorrect, but forgivable. It used to grate my nerves to no extent that we were confused for one another, but with the way things are, I'm happy to be remembered at all these days. Because increasingly, people think I'm a perky Goth girl, bag of bones, or don't exist at all-

Yes! I hear a faucet coming on. It's time for someone's morning shower. Where the f*ck is my camera?

Remember, dear mortal. We are watching you.

Just not in the ways you expect.

No one takes me seriously anymore. Where is the trembling in fear at my name? The terror that once shone so clear in mortal eyes has been replaced by the dull bovine gaze of ignorance. My brethren and I have been reduced to decorating kitschy Hallmark cards and half-assed representations in the media. "Touched By An Angel" my a**. The only touching I'm liable to do is fondle you, if you're a hot little piece of lady-meat. And of course, there's that whole separating the soul from the body business. But I'd much sooner f*ck a Gorgon than save a pious human from a car that's about to burst into flames or alert Mrs. Christian Housewife that Little Timmy is about to run into oncoming traffic with a divine tap on the shoulder. After watching too much daytime television and browsing the Internet, I've come to the sickening conclusion that most humans think angels have nothing better to do than pop into mortal's lives and miraculously save them from burning buildings or being stranded with a broken down car.

Allow me to tell you a cold truth. Beyond your overworked guardian angel, the majority of the angelic host doesn't give a damn about you. You're just a hairless ape in an out-of-the-way galaxy in a remote corner of the universe. Only the lowest and worst-performing angels get assigned to this galactic backwater. Your guardian angels sit around celestial pubs swiping stories of what their idiot charges did that day and griping about their low pay.

Sure, there are important mortals we pay attention to, ones with divine work to do and a higher calling. There are holy men, scholars of renown, and mortal leaders we take a vested interest in. Those amongst you worthy of giving a rat's a** about may have angels guiding and watching over them. I even have a few mortals I'm fond of. But there is a dark side to this patronage. Our chosen mortals must walk a difficult path. Their lives are often a constant struggle, as there is much work to do if you are one of heaven's chosen. Making this world a better place is a near-impossible task, when so many of your own kind are set against you.

Okay. I admit it. I'm a lying cynic. You're all important, and we care about every one of you little filths. We are watching over you, and if you call on us, we'll likely help you, or at least contemplate doing so. Even b*stards like me give a sh*t. But you guys sure do a lot to royally piss us off, especially me. As if being the Angel of Death isn't hard enough, you whine and fight the whole way through, making the death process even more infuriating. I'm doing you a favor, devil damn it! Do you want your soul to stay locked up in a rotting corpse? I didn't think so. But it would make my job a heck of a lot easier.

If you can't tell, I'm drunk as hell at the moment. Whatever. I'm off to go watch Desperate Housewives . Have fun digesting, or whatever it is you humans do...

MADE LOVE TO HIS HELL

I lusted after the knife.
Lucifer stood above me in the laboratory, a scalpel at hand. He was dripping wet with anesthesia, fumigating the room with the heat of his golden body. Blonde hair like drowning sirens set to

serenade Odysseus spooled down the nape of his neck like a net. The elixir of his drugs was setting in - the medium rare steak he hand-fed me, the Malbec from Napa Valley, the tenderloin cut of meat clinging to my arteries like clogging porridge.

I was languorous in his arms. He took a marker, tracing exorcism lines over me, the frankincense spice of his skin and cold metallic taste of his drugs setting into my bones like poison. The aromatics of the incense were hallucinogenic, heightening the state of my emotions and phantasmagorias. Bloodletting, bloodliving. His wings were bound and crooked, odd white feathers sticking out at upended angles.

"You're beautiful when you're my slave, Eve," he purred, chainsmoker's voice like chocolate thunder, a great rumbling in the distance. He walked with a limp - his right ankle to match my broken left foot, from the Nachash's bite.

"Master, make due with haste," I teased, my breasts blossoming under his thumb. He took the hilt of the scalpel and toyed with my left nipple, sucking at the right with his fangs.

Then, as he was ministering to me, and I began to feel warm fire build in the pit of my belly like a serpent's coil, he traced the blade across my inner thigh, knicking it in a Tawu Cross. The Mark of Cain. My immortal, queenly blood flowed, and he set the scalpel down, parting my thighs and nestling his head at the crook of my sex to drink the Edenic Eucharist.

"Elohai nashema Chavah," he prayed, intoxicated, drunk off my mind, body, and life. The blood flowed in rivulets onto his tongue. He supped like an infant drinking milk, rubbing my clit with his free hand.

"It feels so good," I cried out, gyrating under his taloned thumb. He took his bloody mouth and began to eat me out, roving catsrough forked tongue penetrating my inner chamber, pressuring my G spot. I bucked under his chains, my ankles and wrists bound, my neck in a choking collar.

Lucifer gripped me like I was the most miserable sinner in the world. He set the choking collar to strangle deep inhalations with his fist - I could only drink in light breaths. Then, after I came from his ministrations, he slid atop me like an asp, his broken, bandaged wings hulking masses. There was fire in his cinnamon eyes, like Kentucky whiskey.

"Eve, I need you," he groaned, clicking his tongue. His mouth roamed the crook of my neck, his hands playing with the lush rise of my stomach - tiger's stretch marks from birthing our son Arial - and he shucked off his pants, letting the anesthesia settle onto my skin. It flooded my senses - Catholic incense and anhedonia. I would forsake all altars to worship at his

throat. I grasped his hands - as much as my bound, shackled palms would allow - and his divine rod entered me like a horse cock.

He moaned, then bit my neck like Dracula, sucking at the blood that flowed like wine. He smelled of Jean Gatreau and roses. I winced, spasming below as my tight canal let his throbbing cock in. He set a slow tempo, mezzesoprano, and I milked him, my vagina spasming. He let out an echoed sob, and we rutted like wild beasts.

Suddenly, Lucifer took his hands and foot talons and unlashed my bindings. He bent me over his knee and spanked me, then plunged his thumbs into my thigh and neck wounds. I cried out in alto tenulations, and he smacked my ass so hard it bruised, choking me all the while.

Finally, he laid me out sweetly, and eased his huge pink cock into my throat, a slight upward bend to it to give pleasure. I sucked and moaned, fingering myself as he played with my breasts. I pinched his nipple - the left one, his favorite - and he came in spasming gold jism.

Spent, we laid down on the dissection table. I mounted him, carving alien languages on his back with the scalpel. I drank his black blood in turn, and soon, he wilted into a rotten corpse. Alive, but in undeath - all life sucked dry from him by my womb. I mounted the mummy, grinned, and made love to his hell.

THE BOOK OF BARAQUIEL

In the Land of Nod fruits were plentiful, if bruised, and fragrant rains often poured. We watered our gardens, our trees, through a maze-like irrigation system that Forbearer Adam had taught

Grandmason Cain, and Cain passed down to us. I recited my morning song, invoking my patron goddess Asherah:

"Oh, the fabled Cainites— whom Yah's favored Sethites hate! Our men of renown, bound to the earth and her green yields, worshipping at the altar of strange gods. Mammon— industry; Moloch— empire; the port wine-stain feathers shaped like wings of rawhide upon our scarlet backs! 'Industrious Cainites, cavort for us— wilt thou part the bloodied rose?' the kings of foreign lands plead, "Dance the whip and flaming sword! Show us what sin is sweet on your tongue. Kiss away our sorrows and wipe away our tears, sweet Kohonet daughters of Cain!"

I accompanied the morning ritual to Asherah as dawn broke with the clash of my cymbals, naked at her altar enriching her sanctuary of beauty and fertility. My magick rippled throughout Nod, blessing both harvest and land, and I went to my palatial bedroom connected to Asherah's inner chambers to ready for the morning.

"Sweet Lady, give me patience to deal with my little cousins, Istehar and Naamah," I sighed, making a Tawu over my heart with thumb and middle fingers interlocked in an X. Lazily, I admired my wing-shaped birthmark in the mirror as I clothed myself in a gray layered dress, stitched with pomegranates interred within black, Egyptian glass beads. My aerial port wine-stains were shaped like an owl's, spread from my elbows in fine feathery traces up to the nape of my neck. It was the fabled mark us Cainites bore; but to keep off misfortune or to attract it, I was never sure.

"I hate early mornings," I sighed, "I have a feeling in my bones that the foundations of our world will shake. Perhaps High Priest Elizander is gambling heaven and earth with that errant angel again? I hope papa has not lost more money over craps or scarab races with them, dear Lady!" Papa owned a great temple and ten-thousand-cubit estate on the outskirts of Ken ha Gadol; it was the Kingdom of Nod's finest palace, save his brother's matriarchal sanctuary the Kohonet, ruled under the thumb of the wizened Rahab.

"Oh crap, I was distracted! I forgot the last part in my invocation for rain," I sighed, preparing myself as I sang an old song I had learned from Nod's High Priestess, Rahab, Queen of the Kohonet:

Mammon, empire! They are men of renown, the Canaanites! Men of giant stature, men of sages and might— their women of beauty, science, and song! As comely and brave as bulls the maidens all, as sandstone skinned as the great wind-worn sculptures in the desert!

I was summoning the old gods of the blood, as was my duty as Lady of Ken ha Gadol, and the spirits scraped at the back of my skull like a crow pecking pomegranate seeds. My patriotism swelled, and with war gathering on the horizon I shrilly cried the last verse in a toga that held both a ripe fig and bottle of wine, ready to loose red juice and blood at any moment, beating my breast in a frenzy that would make the First Architect Cain proud:

Life in Nod is sweet, as sweet as gristle on bone. Scorned of all Creation the Canaanites are, yet blessed by the Sitra Achra! Watch our demons cavort! Sing of our many conquests! Name the line of Kohonet priestesses and kings! Atop snowy Mount Zephon, watch as we topple the sky!

Only the Assyrians could rival our cruelty; the Egyptians, our majesty; the Minoans, our mystery.

I sent breakfast to Elizander as I wandered out to Asherah's orchard at our palace at the base of Mount Zephon. Alisha of Chavah's seed I was, she who was Samael's beloved; I was a Kohonet-trained priestess, formed in the crucible of sisterhood, of blood, bark, and wine. Under Queen Rahab my birthmark had blossomed, and the secrets of Asherah— as well as serving the nation— had been drummed into my head like the thump of a war-drum.

"How is breakfast, my Alisha?" papa asked while a servant brought us garlic, herb omelets, challah, and dates. I drizzled honey on a loaf, drinking it down with some saffron tea. The fine brick walls of our home had high ceilings with windows made of costly Egyptian glass that, when opened, let drafts of sweet oasis air in. "Wonderful, papa. Say, does the High Priest have need of me today?" I asked, yawning.

Papa smiled. He had a face scarred by a Sethite prince's sword, but was otherwise greying and handsome. After mama's passing, papa took a harem, yet never remarried—she had been his one true love. I tried to stay clear of his consorts.

"Keep an eye on the Watcher atop Mount Zephon, Elizander says."

I nodded, my mood souring. Things were changing, east of Eden: Watchers made camp atop mountains by the smatterings of cities and towns that ringed King Ahrand's country, his holdings, like glimmering rubies. Cymballed Naamah led them, alongside peerless, virginal Istehar, with their lovers Azazel and Samyaza. Oh, how I despised my impish, coquettish cousins!

The Watcher of our town, Baraquiel, had set up camp on Mount Zephon, above the ornate, carved cave where hoary High Priest Elizander so divined. We entertained my Uncle, King Ahrand and Cousins Naamah and Istehar often; I did not have to work the land: I could have gone into the Kohonet like smiling Naamah and gorgeous, virginal Istehar if I wanted.

"Sister Alisha, come dance with us! Your hair is the reddest of us all, like flame across an amber night. We shall teach you the secrets of Lady Lilith and her starry Lilim, where there are men of pleasure and Watchers to delight our every wicked craving. Why, just yesterday Azazel crushed malachite into a fine powder to paint my bronzed lids, and for Istehar, Samyaza fashioned a bracelet of onyx and polished jewels to affix over her tanned wrist," Naamah had burbled; they were always begging me to join them.

I shook my head, remembering their incessant prattling last week— oh, goddess forbid I had to play hostess to them again!

I sat idly by after having finished harvesting palms, fruits, and nuts, as my labor on the estate farm was done for the day and my midwife's herbs dutifully replenished; Elosha, my childhood best friend, was to give birth the town over next week according to her moon chart. And without warning there came a great wind racking up golden dust in the damp soil, shaving scruff from the wheat. I looked beside me to find that I was not alone at my favorite fretting place; the Worry Rock, as I called it. No, there was an angel, an angel of might and of

handsome mien to boot; he wore skin in midnight's particular hue, eyes that shone like lapis lazuli, and was decorated with luxurious curls of white-turquoise hair that fell to his waist in braids. The angel held an astrolabe in his hands, charting the early morning stars that had stubbornly refused to set.

"To what do I owe the honor, introverted Watcher?" I teased. Our town misfit angel, Baraquiel, kept to himself; it was said he abhorred women and had refused every temptation Samyaza and Azazel had lured him to the Kohonet with. As for us humans, Baraquiel would only talk in whispers to High Priest Elizander. The fact that I was, in my dirtied state, the first woman he had probably laid eyes on in years, mattered very much to me.

I had my vanity, after all.

"Rain is coming today. Lightning strikes. It boils my blood, stirs my wings to ride aback the wings. That is the problem of sin, comely daughter of Chavah— Azazel's wings are withered, having strayed too far from the Father, and Samyaza rots not long behind." I crossed my legs, admiring his wings— ibis, like I saw on trips to Egypt with papa. "And yet, Samael and Lilith are still whole, and they have flown long after leaving Yah's paternal court," I pronounced.

Baraquiel winced. "Do not speak to me of the ways of God: you are a heathen. What would you know of my Father?" His inquisition rent my heart into ire and iron, and I rebuked him.

"Quite a lot, actually: I'm a Kohonet-trained qodeshah. I tend the sanctuary of Asherah, and nurse her sacred groves. I midwife babes, heal the sick and heal the lame with my sacred herbs and unguents, dancing for our kingdom's rains." Baraquiel smiled. His teeth gleamed sharply, his midnight skin shining starlike with dew. "Isn't qodeshah what Father's humans call whores?" I winced. "That is not the heart and soul of our practice, Baraquiel. Indeed, we tend to the men once a year at the Festival of Atargatis, turning away neither ugly nor old, sick nor poor from our patient breasts. That is how Lilith and Chavah love: given freely, humbly, like mothers— their suitors as if their own kin. The Sethites gossip a lot, but their lies about Cainites are rumors: they hold neither sting nor vinegar."

Baraquiel twisted one of his intricate braids, laden with bronze beads. "So, then, would you not turn me away?" I blushed, and Baraquiel looked at me hungrily, like a lion waiting to pounce.

"It is many moons until the Festival of Atargatis...but I would be happy to show you Asherah's grove."

"You want me, Alisha. It is etched in sinful Cainite daughter's bones to tempt angels. Why I signed that pact with damnable Azazel is repugnant to me. 'Take a wife,' he said, but the Kohonet was stifling— all those oudh-clad ladies barely clothed? Not like you, Alisha. That dress— it suits you well. Stately. Modest. Good for farming— good, in fact, for flying."

"I do not want you!" I blushed, but I was certain he always saw me admiring him from my palace chambers as he made his daily walk to High Priest Elizander, where they gambled over dice; playing craps with a cantankerous, wheezing elder was not how I imagined I would spend eternity, if given the chance. Once, Baraquiel and father had raced scarab beetles. Papa lost and refused to see Baraquiel again; I could surmise papa forfeited quite a sum of money. In the morning Baraquiel appeared jolly at Elizander's door with casks of fine Minoan wine, and by then it was not hard to guess where papa's money went.

Baraquiel smirked. "You are a qodeshah, my Alisha. A heathen. It does not matter what you want, does it? It only matters what Azazel and Naamah deem you fit for."

I scowled. "You are coarser than sand, Baraquiel, and are ignorant of our ways. I'll let it be known that I have never done a dance with a Watcher."

"Not even shy Samyaza?"

"That lunatic is just pining after closed-leg, prissy Istehar! I can't stand the lot of them! Naamah is spoiled, and Istehar is a shrew."

"And I cannot stand my fallen brothers. So what does that make us, dearest Alisha?"

"In a pickle."

"I like to eat pickles; they are one of humanity's finest creations. That does not sound so bad."

We were leaning against each other by now, some sort of animal magnetism drawing us together, or simply us bonding over both being irascible, ornery bastards. I was not too sure which it was.

"Where does an angel get pickles from, Baraquiel?" "Elizander makes them. You really should talk to him more. He is wise. In fact, just yesterday he told me how to ingest Syrian rue so as to experience strange visions."

"You're doing drugs with an old man?" I laughed. "What did you mean, then, when you said 'my dress was made for flying'?"

Baraquiel smiled. "Shall I show you, Alisha?" He lifted me gently but sturdily into the air as we set off flying. The air was sweet, warm, and thick, the clouds damp but not clinging, and his great ibis wings spread out like war flags.

"I could get used to this, Baraquiel."

"Call me Baraq."

We took to playing craps with Elizander.

Over time, I built up stamina to visit Baraquiel's camp atop Mount Zephon. Always, we went flying, and over time, he fell from the stars for me like Lucifer struck down from heaven, in love with a comely daughter of Cain. We worshipped Asherah and danced for Samael, and made love for Lilith and Chavah. I found myself with child by the third month, and Baraquiel dropped his pickle mid-bite out of sheer joy.

"I will have to be a little more careful when you fly, then."

The rains came that night with a loud thunderstorm, filling Nod's wells for years to come. The canals were brimming with fertile waters, freshly churned soil, and loam. Baraquiel, the angel of lightning, was like a weathervane, the winds responding to his moods. We made plans to marry, and Rahab blessed us on our first journey to the Kohonet together. Naamah was ripe with her second child, and Azazel lingered at the edges like a black ink-stain, scheming.

That night, Baraquiel's feathers began to fall out, one by one, like snow atop Mount Zephon.

By the fifth month, my husband had Elizander cauterize his dead ibis wings from his back.

"Where I'm going, as father to the fruit of my seed, I won't need any marks of my old pact with Yah," Baraquiel simply said, caressing my swollen womb as I cried over his lost bit of heaven.

Samyaza had finally had enough of Istehar refusing his advances; she asked him the Secret Name of Yah, escaping his assault by flying to the stars. Yah, taking pity on one of the Cainites for what might have been the first time in eternity, changed Istehar into a constellation. They came to call her the Star Maiden. Samyaza hung himself the next morning, and Yah made his death a starry tomb; you may know him as Kesil the Hangman. What it took for an angel to die, I did not wish to know.

The Nephilim, our children with the Watchers, grew fast if they were conceived out of lust, not out of love. Baraquiel and I heard rumors every day that they were giants, full-grown in a year, and Azazel and Naamah were setting their scions and the Kohonet's other half-angel offspring as lords over our enemy the Sethites. And then the Nephilim turned on Nod.

First the Nephilim ate the cattle. Then they ate the sheep. Finally, the goats and pigs. When even that was not enough, the Nephilim turned on man. Azazel and Rahab had lost control, and the Land of Nod fell into misrule and infamy. Elizander, papa, his consorts and servants, Baraquiel, Elusha's family and I fled to Egypt, carrying as many riches as we could to start life anew, and just in time at that, for

Raphael was sent to bind the Watchers hand and foot in Dudael.

After that, Samael sent a flood, a great drowning of his son Grandmason Cain's land, to wipe the Nephilim off the face of the earth.

All but one.

I gave birth to a girl with ibis wings, lapis lazuli eyes, amber skin, and red hair: Sarai. Elusha was her godmother, and we cut her wings like the Sethites circumcise their children.

Baraquiel has taken to dyeing his white-turquoise hair with henna. We work as scribes and gardeners, and I serve as a priestess of Qadesh— the name of Asherah in this foreign land. Every year I serve my goddess. I turn away no man, young or old, Greek or Egyptian or Sethite, African or Assyrian. But it is a bitter service, and all I can do is think of Baraquiel, my dear husband, as the strangers ruthlessly spear into me from above.

One day, in our large house by the Nile, Sarai was playing with seashells, and I looked over at Baraquiel— still beautiful, but more mortal than he had ever been— and I squeezed his hand, asking him "Was it worth it? Leaving Heaven, leaving your holy post atop Mount Zephon, taking a heathen bride?"

Baraquiel smiled like it was the most obvious, pleasing answer in the world. "My darling, beautiful Alisha, is it worth it to spend months brining a pickle? Does rendering the common, humble cucumber into a treasure for the tongue not take some patience sacrificed, and tempers tried? Are you not my greatest service of all?"

And with that, we kissed, drank wine, and called over our darling little Sarai to enjoy a plate of dates. She pecked her papa on the cheek and told us stories about her doll. When I looked into Baraquiel's eyes I saw the crackle of joyous lightning.

Love, true love, is often hard to find. But I lived in the Land of Nod once, wiped from the face of the earth, and I myself won a husband from the stars. Strange, us forgotten Cainites. Foreign in our magic, sinful in our ways.

Proud people, though, the memory of Nod.

And for Asherah?

I dance.

THE HEART OF G-D IS DARK AND DEEP

It was Christmas Eve. Rain fell as Michael drank a beer in Scott's Edition. It was a Double IPA and he had just finished using the rain to wash off some fucking Nephil brat demon gore Samael had sired on yet another VCU art student slut. Probably some

weed whore that prostituted herself out to his twin
- the King of Rot and Shadow—for some satvia.

Now, Michael didn't like to mix his suppliers with
family. The weed Samael offered Michael was never
bought. He planted it on the bodies of the women
Michael executed as God's Right Hand that had
dared fuck an angel. Only demons and the unclean
bought weed off his fucker of a brother.

Michael's weed from Samael were serial killer
gifts.

Now Ha-Satan could tempt. And Ha-Satan could
while. But like Dexter, Samael also collected samples
from the human whores he fucked.

Little toes, always chopped off them after they
had delivered the child, and Samael had stolen the
Nephil brat away to age in Moloch's clone vats with
Samael's genes into shadowside Satanic golems.
Besides Emet, Samael put toes in the Nephil golem
ears – always the left pinkie. Little unhinged love
notes to the Son of God. Michael unrolled the last
one. It was Akkadian, a line of furrowing a woman's
mound like good soil. Ishtar and Dumuzi or some
raw ass pagan shit.

Michael downed the beer – too skunky – in one
fetid, holy gulp.

"Bartender, just a Corona."

"This is a gourmet ecobrewery. We don't serve
corporate shit."

Michael summoned his holy petersword from the
ether, blacked out reality around the hipster bitch

bartender and him, and siphoned the edge of the blade through her right gauge, then plucked.

Blood, hanging ear off like his old beloved fuckbuddy and Chosen One, Peter.

"Do I have to ask, darling?" Michael said kindly, voice dripping with southern gentility.

She wept softly, clutching her ear. "You're a monster."

"God, you mean. Get me that Corona."

Satan – Samael – was out schmoozing at the meadery. It was Black Heath. He stank of cheap Indian food and women's piss. Cuban cigar, sharp lips. Michael was drunk off his ass, and stumbled over to Black Heath.

"Akkadian, really?"

"Yeah, whatever Mike. Like the bitch I fucked? She's a blonde. Like your Joan. Little present for you, asswipe."

"Stop fucking the mortals, Sam."

Samael's red viper eyes slit to poison, and his black asp curls writhed like Medusa. Lucifer Rebelling.

"Stop fucking with me, Mike, and stop lusting after fucks with me."

"I'll fucking dogshit murder you if you sire another Nephil."

"Then what, fuck my corpse again and wait until handy old Father old fashions me into revival, and I end up waking up from the Abyss with your rancid gold dick in my ass? Midas' touch, you both have.

And you have angel lust. Never did like the girls, Michael. The only girl in your garden, you cut off her hair and made wear armor, then when she kissed you, left and had burned at the stake. You were so repulsed, a woman's touch. You're too Roman. Like your fucking Vatican, diddler of altars boys. I was the first altar boy. Lucky how that ended, Father kicking me out cause I wasn't some prepubescent ephebe slutshow taking it up the ass from Metatron anymore-"

Michael slapped him. Samael bit. Michael punched and strangled. Samael kicked.

Michael kissed. Samael groaned. Out of Richmond, out of the alley of the oversweet alcohol, mead on Michael's lips, some shit Corona and lime on Samael's.

The truth, left better to the sages. This was a dirty fuck.

They went to the Cave of the Bees. Where Adam and Eve were buried. Fucked on Eve's grave, dug up her corpse and played with her ribs. Lucifer licked her skull, threading the pink serpent tongue out her jaw, placing it on Michael's dick to suck him off, pretending it was Eve's blowjob.

"Fancy the women now, Mike?" Lucifer hissed, eyes now burning blue. Michael was gold, all gold, all brass and polish and lighthouse. Samael was pale as the moon.

"Shut the hell up and kiss my balls, fuckface."

Samael bit them.

"Ouch, you fucking rotting pigshit bastard. Those toes had been rancid fly food for a month. How do you pick your whores Sam?"

"Blondes. Blondes give the best head, like you. Your skulls are empty, more room for my huge, girthy dick you want in your mouth-

Michael wrestled Samael like Jacob at the foot of Peniel. The rabbis never knew if Samael or Michael had blessed Esau or Jacob, who had the more cursed life, after all? Some bitch wife Leah, sons that sold off Joseph. Maybe it was better to be a reject and redhead and eat pottage in rot all your days.

Michael shoved his shining, burning foot onto Lucifer's face, crushed his jaw until Lucifer was nothing but a bloody pulp. Samael moaned, jerking himself off as Michael stomped and stomped.

"M-o-r-e, holy boy."

Michael took his ass, breaking his hips with violent thrusts. Samael was just whipcord, tall, pale snake. Michael was always the buff lion, Aslan or some shitshow sold to little children: No, God never made the whale swallow Jonah. No, God loves all creatures. No, God doesn't cut the clits off half the women in Africa and the Middle East.

No, angels don't fuck. Especially the Left and Right Hand. Hands are only meant to jerk off the Father, not a handshake, which is technically what Michael and Samael were doing.

Michael came in the bloody pulp of Lucifer's broken limbs. His seed, burning, shoved the soul out of Samael and into the Abyss, pouring out his lacerated intestines into Eve's corpse. Eve bloomed into life again, a mewling baby, from the holy seed of God.

"Shut up, Samael's first whore," Michael sighed, weary, cradling the baby. He nursed her with some of Samael's gore, kissed her cheek – repulsion, even at a girl this small, like that fetid creature Joan kissing his stubbled cheek. He had tried. He had taken the shame of flame. But the rot grew, and she did not

Look

Like Sam.

Michael ate Eve, then vomited the baby bones. Lucifer gasped back to life with the digested carapace of his first and only love, Eve. Lilith was way too fucking lesbian with Agrath and Eistheth and Naamah, after all. And Eve was a lousy fuck, the way Sam liked them. Easy to control.

"You killed and ate her. Funny. You know, I saw Noah in the Abyss. He's building an Ark for the disembodied Nephilim I always summon in the clones of my sons with those Richmond whores. Trying to pull a bosom of Avram and save them. It's some kind of new plan, more soldiers from Heaven. He told me I'm serving God even by making bastard sons. I told him, you were the first bastard Son of God, Christ-Michael. Wouldn't bastards be the best anyway? Then Noah spat at my feet, and I cut out his eyes. Lucky that, regenerating with Mary's tending. She's no good with eyes, can't even help poor Lucy."

"I hate myself, Lucifer." Michael cried, sobbing, collapsing in Lucifer's arms.

Lucifer-Samael held Michael-Christ, tender, sang B'shem HaShem to him.

"I love you, Michael. More than you'll ever know. Let's go get some Thai. Night sweats and night fucks and night kills make me want curry."

So Michael dried his tears on Samael's Armani, donned some Valentino, and they went to Manhattan, but sadly ended up going to Serafina. The Thai dive was full of vampires and elves, not a crowd angels liked to mingle with.

Samael spooned gnocchi into Michael's mouth, Michael curled in his arms like two CEOs in love in some kind of fantasy world where CEOs were not old and gray. The silver viper and the gold.

Michael fed him puttanesca, critiqued the olive quality, and said San Marzano tomatoes were overrated.

"But they're the best, Mike."

"You'd know."

THE KISS OF ATTRITION, BETWEEN
BROTHERS LONG GONE

The Lightbringer attended to his duties.
Idly, he ate a wormy pomegranate, dressed in a white tunic. Black veins ran like a map across his back, spreading to chalk-white shoulders. He

lingered in the shadows, watching the Milky Way canoe toward the outer boundaries of heaven. The stars hung like fireflies above, reflecting off the perfection of his skin as he stood under the boundless moon. The satellite drifted slowly across the hours, and the music of the spheres churned as time's machinations moved the night to day.

Cherubim whirled above, shifting mixtures of man and beast that carried the heavens on their backs. They shepherded the stars, singing in ethereal tones. At a glance they resembled dragons with human faces blossoming from pearly wings. Their backs were shelled like tortoises or jeweled beetle carapaces that upon closer inspection resembled intricate, interlocking armor. One could not discern if their human forms were consumed in biological plating or if they truly were chimeras.

He watched them. Once, that had been his duty, but no more. He softly touched the twin scars that mounted his shoulder-blades. The old red fire of the wound flared. He smirked, then put out the Morning Star - proudest in all the constellations - with his thumb. The planet Venus dimmed, only to blaze into life again when he lowered his hand. He laughed drily and finished the fruit, tossing it over the canyon rim below.

The song of the cherubim lilted. They descended like flaming wheels, swooping down below into the landscape obscured by night. Their voices faded to silence. The angels' chimeric forms resolved into those of men. In hollows of darkness they stood, flesh beginning to glow, then blazed into pillars of light. Each beam rocketed up into the sky to match a star above.

The stars flickered in time with their breaths.

He smiled at his brothers' devotion as his chest began to thrum like a drumbeat. The skin over his heart glowed blue-white, burning with sweet agony. He contained a scream that would have rose to ragged ululations of ecstasy, just as each of his brothers held their tongues.

Gritting his teeth, he let his glory pour forth. It seared, the substance of divinity firing upward to Venus. His mind was consumed; he let the waves of pain rush against him like water crashing to shore. The frothing foam scattered memories like sea glass: his Father's hands in his, teaching him to shape the cosmos to his will. His fingers on the locks of a yellow-haired girl, braiding them meticulously with roses. He recalled how his hands had fumbled then, picking the thorns off for her before wending the vines between the golden strands. He had had no callouses then, no scars-

The fires of the heavens roared like a waterfall. The sun was on the verge of rising. His pain intensified. He closed his eyes, clasping his hands in prayer.

Hands told stories; some said they determined fate. A heart line slashed across a palm spoke of love, a six-lined star meant protection. The meanings, for mortals, were endless.

His hands were blank. The only marks on his skin were the ones he had earned. "Where is your fate line?" she had asked long ago, laughing.

"Fate line? I have none, Eve."

"That is a pity. How can you choose your destiny, if you have no guide to it?" She traced the absence of his palms.

He flexed his pinions. "I have my wings- that is enough."

She touched their snowy whiteness. "Flying is one thing, brother, but without a map, where will you go?"

"I know where I am going, child. Some paths are best left unknown."

But he had strayed down shady roads in the coming eons, and the pearly wings grew to not be enough.

One evening, he tried drawing delicate curves on his palms with her sewing needles. Over and over he dug them, deeper into his flesh, until the needles stuck through his hand. Each time they healed, devoid of scars. She caught him unawares and screamed when she saw him.

"Not like this!" she had howled, plucking the needles from his palms and bandaging him with torn strips of her dress. She ran her fingers through his hair, hands so soft and cool against his temple they could be milk. So small he could enfold them like a butterfly, which he did. He steadied her shaking, afraid she would crack like a doll. "This is my fault," she wept as he rocked her. "You have no need of stupid fate lines. Your wings are enough to guide you. Can't you see how whole you are? I am not. I was jealous of you, brother, jealous! You are the prince of the angels, have all and I have nothing. I am made of dust and sorrow; I walk through the dirt and mud. Father regrets me - he damns my curiosity, I, who was merely made to revel in creation. I am a broken thing: I go against my nature in craving to create what I am meant to enjoy. Ever since we were expelled from Eden, I cannot read the damned things on my hands."

He clasped her hands in his, wings enfolding her. "I can," he whispered, "and you are the most whole thing I have ever known."

"You can read them?" she asked weakly. "What do they say?"

"They say that you are the wisest of all creatures, Eve, and that nothing I have done is your fault. That in you lies the fire of a million generations. The only fate we control is our own."

Her gaze could still the ocean: "Then promise me you will never do anything that hurts you, ever again, Lucifer. Promise me you will be gentle as you have always been and treat yourself with the same care you give me."

"I promise, Eve. Though I would not call myself gentle-"

She silenced him with a kiss, both ignoring that the way their paths were headed, it was a promise he would not keep. He recalled how he had cupped her face like it was manna. His hands, entwined in her hair -

The sun crept closer to the rim of the horizon. His heart scorched, ribs burning in his chest. Tears welled in his eyes. Those hands, which he would now shudder to place on her snowy flesh, broke their fervent prayer.

He examined them, removed. They profaned all they touched, sullied with the stains of ages. Blood, tears, piss, plagues. Yet no matter what he did, they remained clean. His brothers were all the same. Try as they might, they could not write their own stories. All they did was erased from their skin.

Their fates had been determined for them. The only scars they were allowed to keep were those earned at ultimate cost.

The stars blotted out one by one, waiting. He flexed his fingers. Once, the slender digits had brought life to mortal lips. Now they drew souls out of mouths. Just like he had cast off one name for another, he had traded purposes after the Fall:

"No," he had pleaded, tears in his eyes. "My name is Lucifer. The bright and morning star." "And now it is Samael, the poison and venom of God. Your gifts will be suffering and death." "No! I am the Lightbringer!"

"And now that light would burn you. Death cannot bear life. You killed her in your folly! To repeat that would be madness-"

"I am beyond madness and your wretched salvation, Michael. Do not offer me repentance. I was trying to save her. I will save her! What is dead can be brought back to life. Eve's soul is mine, mine."

"You damned her from the moment she met you."

He roared her name in agony. The Morning Star stood belfry to the first rays of sun. Pain forgotten, he was lost in the onslaught of his mind.

Hell is not a place, but the past. He carried it with him always. The angels below were lost in their own tortures. They pleaded their cases before the sun. Perhaps, this morning, they would be forgiven. For his brothers were each of them fallen, bereft of their Creator, alone.

The sun rose in judgment, washing out the light of the Morning Star. He screamed and doubled over as his flesh seared to the bone. The penetrating rays licked him the clean white bone of the Reaper, rendering him into a skeleton. He saw with eyes that were black hollows, and rose to embrace the deadly radiation.

The landscape pooled before him. A red desert raced out to brimming golden mountains, where dawn gently lapped over the ruins of a once magnificent city. It was carved into the cliff faces like Petra, inhospitable to humans. No steps or bridges connected the towering

abodes - sheer drops followed the open doors - and there were none of the comforts of civilization, merely bare floors dusted with wildflowers. The fallen angels shook below as they prayed, flesh peeling as their blood pooled on the ground. Wind stirred the sand into molten plumes, like hourglasses in reverse, grains snaking through fallen pillars and stories upon stories of sandstone. It buffeted him, sliding between his ribs. A great thundering came from the distance.

"Welcome, brother," he murmured as the solar angel stirred to his vigil. Soon, a figure shadowed the sun. Michael landed atop the sere cliff, facing his twin. "Time to slay the beast," the Morning Star said.

Tears were in Michael's eyes. "You know this is never necessary, Samael." He laid his weapons at his twin's feet.

"Your sword, dear brother, through the neck. Or the heart, if you prefer. I seem to lack one, I suppose. A downside to being bone-"

"Why, day after day, do you torment me with this?" The question hung like the gallows over their heads. "Our brothers below us are suffering. Above us, they are weeping. All Heaven and Hell become one, and you prolong it with your murder."

"It is yours too, my twin," he said, almost tender. The bone-man walked to Michael's side, dabbing at the tears with his claw hands. "Damn these things," he said, looking at his fingers in disgust. "I have had too much time alone with my palms."

"In that we may find solidarity. Mine tire of bearing weapons. If you would only quit your stubbornness, the War would end immediately."

"If only it were that simple. I always envied you your straightforward thinking. Whose load is heavier, brother: the Lightbearer, or he who bears the sword? One's burden is insubstantial-"

"Enough with your damn riddles!" Michael roared, slapping the skull's cheek. "Repent! Come home, brother. Be whole."

Samael's hand lingered on his smarting jawbone. "No."

Michael took his brother's shoulders in his hands. "Each day you pray for forgiveness, and we grant it to you. Then you reject it. You - all of you!-" he yelled across the canyons, down at the fallen ones, silver tears in his emerald eyes, "-choose suffering over redemption. Why, my brother? Why?"

"Because, Michael. It is our lot. The suffering, the scars, make us whole. There is no going back to Eden."

"I know," whispered Michael, sorrowful, "but I can hope." He embraced his brother slowly, shaking, and kissed his bony brow.

"What is dead cannot be brought back to life, as you said so long ago. Look at me as I truly am," Samael laughed drily. "Such a prince of angels I would make. No, that path is now yours, and your halo is ill-suited for me. The only crown fitting me is one of thorns." He lifted Michael's sword and pressed it to his ribs. "For her?" Samael asked gently.

Michael obliged. In a scene old as time, he slayed the beast, killing the darkness which would rise once more next evening, only to be slaughtered come morning tithe. Over and over they engaged in the battle, trapped in their own hells, hearts torn asunder anew. Samael had died many times - in truth, he craved it. As the Angel of Death, it was him. Each time, it brought him closer to her- in the blackness he could feel her, the hollow emptiness of his heart that marked her unknown grave.

Broken, Michael pushed him over the edge. Gabriel trumpeted above. The earth opened like a great maw to swallow him up.

"Eve," Samael called softly, plummeting into the abyss. The ground sucked the fallen angels down into the pit, denying them God's saving grace. In their fall, they burned proud.

Michael wiped his blade clean of rot. The tithe was paid.

The day was born.

FRENCH LADIES

Eve spread out her golden form for me like a
Picasso, all streaks of limb and red sex wound.
"Lilith, is this the right angle?" she teased coyly,
my wife spreading her pudenda apart with ring'ed
fingers – bands for demons, bands for angels, just

like I – splitting her folds apart so I saw L'origine du Monde.

I licked my horsehair brush, then did a bold slash of oil across my cloth canvas. "Every angle is like a wicked fruit with you, my darling," I cheered, sipping some Pinot Noir as I gazed at Eve, in the nude.

Our chalet – where we got away from our husbands in the outskirts of Normandy – storm-glimmered with rain through the French doors. The cozy cottage-meets-Art Deco aesthetique of our palatial suite was also a home for wayward souls – those still clinging on to earthly attachments, children, mothers, sons, husbands – not ready for the afterlife.

Eve and I made galettes and kimchi pancakes, masala chai and Swedish meatballs, cooking to our heart's delight for the children of us – the Sons and Daughters of Lilith and Eve. Satan and Adamah factored in a bit, but everyone know – the Darklight and Lightdark Mother's love was legendary. Once, long ago, my claws through Eve's breast, her Jeanne d'Arc sword through my thigh – but all that was past.

Eve traced the scar where I had cut the meat of her left tit apart. She toyed with it, biting her lip, inviting me in.

"Let the paint dry, Lily. I hunger."

"I made raspberry torte, sly daughter of G-d."

"And I want your fruit, Lilith Malkira."

"Ten more minutes, angel cake. I drink dry the Lethe when I see your resplendent form, you know, Chavs. All there is to you is music."

"All there is to you is dark angles, fierce Inanna. And blood under nail."

Eve began to toy with the pearl of her womanhood, looking me dead down. Delicious frission and goosebumps curdled my brown flesh, and hunger grew in my mound. I watched as she wetted her fingers with her juices, calling out my name, then inserted the digits slowly but surely between the dark curls of her sex.

I drew it all – that mad passion, that lust and stinking love, madrigal to my terpsichore. Her Callypigean blessings matched my ample bosom, and I turned the canvas around to show her my Matisse-meets-DeGas impression of her.

"Beauty, Lilith. You have such an eye. All I have are my poems."

I shucked off my jodhpurs and leather top and let my black mane loose like a lion. Naked, eagle-footed, owl-winged – my hair shone red in certain lights. I swallowed the stormy night beyond our chateau, and from a far distant room, the servants set out the labors of culinary love Eve and I had done today for the souls: croquettes, latkes, and apple dumplings with kasha.

"Your poems make you the Crown of Creation," I purred, leaning in to kiss Eve. She met my mouth with fierce devotion, biting, sucking, mouthfucking, as she milked my breasts with tender hands. "I – uglgh – love you."

"What shall I do to my Lady Demon today?" Eve asked darkly, her brown chocolate ringlets unfurling onto mine own tresses. She traced her hands down my soft belly, laugh lines, star lines, birth lines from our broods to match her own. Stretchmarks we had tattooed gold and silver on our flesh, alongside Trees of Life on our backs, spiraling out into the upper echelons of the Spheres.

"Make me your slave. Let me lay beneath you."

"Oh, Lilith, laying beneath Woman? How rebellious of the Night Swallower."

She toyed with my sex, fingerfucking me, and sucked at the hollow of my throat. I cried out raggedly, clasping her back, and Eve's Hathor-imbued cow horns. We were goddesses of fertility, birth, and death, and we scissored and kissed and made love to the ages as Baal's lightning pealed.

Afterwards, spent, I lay in the crook of Eve's arm – though she short and plump, I lithe and athletic and columnesque, hooked Jewish nose to her own Romanic aquiline lines and sharp angles, she liked to be

Big Spoon.

She played with my owl wings, brushing them with a special, soft angelhair brush Gabriel had made us one Christmas.

"Remember making love under the shade of the Ziggurat, in those gorgeous gardens, and you always smelled of jasmine as I grew dates and figs?" Eve sighed, closing her eyes and reaching up, up, up to kiss my brow. "I'm so glad we have eternity, Lilith. My love for you burns like Uriel's sword, you know. Nothing can whet it."

I turned in her arms and embraced my wife, breast-bound. "Eve, you are my inspiration."

"Lilith, you are my master. King to my Queen."

We kissed, as of old, as of always, then went
To dinner.

RED WINGS

Blood and ash in my serrated mouth. There were dim lights in the castle - a blonde in a white dress, hair draped like longing across the Persian carpet, with red eyes - nursing me back to health.

She was a familiar face. A spot of love in a glove drawer. She fit onto my wing wounds like a lullaby - I had been plucked, tarred, and feathered, that I knew, spat out of God's foibles like Icarus to fall downward in an arc from Eden, into the Pit.

But this girl - she was no more than nineteen, with white wings - she had a bracelet of jade around her arm, carved like a biting snake. She took an ointment of honey and cloves and pressed it into my battered scars and lacerated back. I howled.

"Who are you? What have you done?" I sobbed. I looked at my hands - black talons, pale flesh like the underside of a snowstorm. I looked wretched, like a killer. "What - what is my name?"

She softened, setting down the poultice and brush she had been painting my back with. Easing me to my side, the starry aureoled blonde's eyes settled to blue. She gave a smile like sunshine and champagne bubbles: "Samael. You're Samael. There was a skirmish at Heaven's Gate - where your brother Michael dealt you a deathly blow." She pet my forehead and my teeth gnashed at her tender touch.

I wanted to drain the blood from her carapace - my cock tightened, why? She was so innocent - so easy to corrupt. I wanted to be inside her, possess her as a demon does his nun, make her speak in Latin and fuck a cross. Such blasphemy as her wide placid eyes glowed with warmth. She laughed.

"You're so predictable, my love," the strange, alluring girl sighed, resting gently her head on my chest to listen to my heart. "Ah, good, it's beating again. That black hole in there - sometimes, if it doesn't get enough of my blood, enough of my heart meat - it drains you of your alma, makes you full of the yetzer ha ra. We can't have your venom poisoning yourself, Sam."

My cock twitched. Damn it, I was naked, I realized. She looked at it tenderly, arcing over me, her breasts expanding in a rosy blush under her white chemise, pink nipples peeking through the translucent fabric. Her gold hair fell in an elegy onto my lap as she traced one hand over the black hairs on my chest... the other lingering on my pink white girthy, humongous dick.

Precum wept. She licked it, smiling. "You need to calm down, Sam. You're in no position for lust."

I shuddered, heaving, the great height of me - was I ten feet tall? Fourteen? No, maybe twelve - dwarfing her five foot nothing form.

"Girl, what is your name? My chest feels like - like it will explode when I hunger - uh, look at you."

I blushed. Blushing was... strange. The crack to my head by a flaming sword was all I remembered. Amnesia, I was sure. But I knew I was King, King of a great Underworld, of steel and blood skies, of crimson waters and markets of pleasure and damnation, of iron mountains, granite steppes, wild hell beasts... and pleasing women.

"Hah, you don't remember? You're always like this after you get knocked on the head. I'm Eve,

Samael, your wife. Well, girlfriend. Maybe we are married... but it's no marriage the Heavens would recognize, and you have Agrath, Eisheth, Lilith, and Naamah to care for... so there is little space left for me. I -" she dizzyed me up with wine and poetry, a carafe of red bitters in hand that smelled of pungent, regal alcohol, which she poured into cups "- am an angel in Hell."

My wings shifted. I screamed as the feathers began to moult as she fed me the wine - it was laced with her blood, I knew now - she was bleeding down her back as she parted her hair, carved feathers on her slender, curved back. She was curvy like a Mother of Life - wait, wasn't she a mother of my Son, Cain?

"Cain!"

"Yes," Eve laughed, tickling my dick. I shoved her onto me reflexively, roving my hands over her huge, ripe breasts and hips so large, they were melons, her wasp waist a pleasing song, with a soft stomach like a woman who enjoyed dessert. "He's fine. Having dinner with his bride Luluwanna."

Dark glory radiated from me as my passerine feathers came in. Gray, sooty owl wings. Dappled like a mare in brown and black shadow over the blue-dun sheen. I wrapped them around her as she straddled my chest, pouring the bloody wine down her tits, down her navel, and having it flow into my mouth.

I hungered. "Eve. I remember. I need you."

Eve smiled like starshine. She pet my brow, the giving mother - my heart, my life, my light. If Lilith was my queen, if Eisheth was my regent, if Agrath was my rod, if Naamah was my dancer - Eve was my shadow. My reflection with no light.

"Ride my face, Eve. Pour the blood wine in your cunt. I'm aching to eat you."

"Oh great serpent," she winked, sitting her weight on my face. Her labia were slick with her wetness, her blonde hairs on her nether lips suffusing me with the musk of her womanhood.

I breathed in as she rubbed her clit against my nose, taking my long, thick, cats rough demon tongue and teasing the folds. She cried out in ecstasy, dribbling my sustenance of her blood and Malbec down her chest, pooling on my face. I wrapped my wings around her in wild abandon and razed her bloody back, shedding gray down as I grew strong from her heady elixir.

Her clit swelled, and I kissed and sucked at her inner and outer labia, then focused on the pearl of her sex, sucking at it, using fangs to gently skim. I used my hands to open up her folds and speared my tongue deep in.

"Fuck! You taste - like - like - fuck!" I crowed, my dick weeping excitement.

Noticing her husband's need, my little cherry tart turned around so her ass was riding my face and began to suck my dick. I cried out to all pendulous gods who dangled salvation like Forbidden Fruit at her and I, then snatched it away at a moment's objection to the cruelty of it all.

She gave head like the angels. Swallowing me balls deep, working the shaft and jewels of Hell. I ate her ass out like it was chocolate cake - it tasted earthy, like the soil she and Adam had sprang from. I plunged my tongue into the rosebud of her anus and she screamed, breathing hot air on the tip of my dick as she held onto my cock for dear life, stroking it, licking it, slobbering all over it as she shrieked.

We fucked like wild wolves, giving head - giving Hell.

The wine and her blood and my feathers painted the silk black sheets in white, red, and gray. When we were done, and that phantasmal exchange of spooky entanglement at the atomic level had paid the piper, I was healed, her back was now scarred, and we settled into twilight.

I cradled her in the mess, drunk, giddy.

"Welcome home again, my Red Sam," Eve grinned, then dozed, her soft snores comforting.

I held my wife like an answer to an elven question, laid her atop my chest, pulled the covers up, and whispered into the seashell of her sleeping ear:

"You are my first and last."

Tenderness seized my chest, but I buried that deep within me.

We could never be anything more... or maybe, we were

all

that
was.

Tartini Appletini

Lucifer surveyed the Garden. It was the season of frost and fire, of hell and damnation. Another bloody scrabble with Michael.

Adam watched him, trying to till the salted earth. Adam eyed Lucifer warily, his gold eyes and blond hair iced in snow. He was dressed in a garment of rawhide, his shovel, clippers, and spade shining metallic in the winter.

Lucifer idly plucked winter berries only fit for birds and angels from Adam's favorite bush - he liked to watch the partridges - and ate the red fruit with his ragged teeth. Adam scowled.

"If you're going to stand there eating my crops, bastard, get to work and plant seeds. You always eat us out of house and home." Adam threw him a bag of apple seeds. It was time to plant them.

"Nothing grows planted by my hands," Lucifer sighed, spitting the last berry out at Adam's shoulder. It bounced off his hard muscle.

"Angels are useless," Adam said, near-pummeling Lucifer with the spade. "Bend over. You always do it for Michael. And put that blasted Adonis body to use. Dig."

"Yes, Master," Lucifer quipped. "I only grow cursed fruit."

"Lu, I am master of the Sefer HaChaim. I have all the armaments and adornments of God, Father of Humanity, master of the black magick of the Sefer Raziel. I enslaved legions of my offspring to serve me. You think I give a rat's ass about cursed fruit?" Adam donned his black robes and began to chant from the Sefer Raziel. Lucifer watched in awe as the sapphire tablet in Adam's hands glowed, summoning spring.

"I suppose I could help," Lucifer sighed. He didn't much like human men. Hairy like Michael. Smelly, too - all that testosterone. Angels went hairless below the brow. Ephebes. Like Grecian statues of Apollo. He dug a tiny hole, palming the seeds, and planted three black dots. "Heh, apples. I like your wife's apples-"

Adam clapped him over the head. Lucifer low swept him, and soon, they were wrestling, cursing each other. The garden began to grow in mad frenzy as Adam's Sefer Raziel floated in the air, summoning the season of virility.

"Don't talk of my wife, asshat," Adam grunted, pinning Lucifer. Lucifer's black hair and blue eyes spooled out under Adam connivingly. With a talon, Lucifer stripped Adam of his black necromancer robes and rawhide. His muscled, tan flesh - blond chest hairs, eyes like brass - were somehow pleasing.

"Like her, I am under you, oh me oh my," Lucifer sighed, tracing Adam's thigh. Adam blushed, noticing the erection between his own thighs.

"I am not a proud man, Lucifer," Adam cursed, pinning Lucifer under him. He undid Lucifer's armor and smacked him on the side of the head with the spade. "You planted three seeds. So I'll fuck you three times. You're lazy as piss, and a sore worker."

"Oh, maybe I was asking for it." Lucifer snatched a winterberry, ate it, then spit it in Adam's face.

Adam's erection needed nursing. Lucifer was happy to oblige. The Father of Men was fun to play with, and Lucifer was a torturous being. Adam gripped Lucifer's head, cursing, bucking into the Devil's tight, wet throat.

Lucifer swirled his long, white tongue over Adam's cock. He milked and pumped and sucked, then finally, after what seemed like an hour, Adam came in thick white spurts, hot and heavy in Lucifer's hand. Lucifer ate it up like whipping cream.

"One and done," Adam grunted, shoving Lucifer under him, spreading his ass cheeks, and taking his hole with his still-hard erection, now slicked with Lucifer's spit.

Lucifer cried out as Adam penetrated him mercilessly. It smelled of earth and rain. Roses and cinnamon bloomed as the men fucked.

"You two are at it again!" came a bright periwinkle laugh. The two froze. "Eve?"

"Yes, it's me, you two fools of husbands." She clapped, amused, in a sundress and Birkenstocks, watering can in hand. "Don't mind me, I'll just watch."

"Join us, wife," Adam commanded. She had to obey.

"I like this kind of work," Lucifer said, sliding his cock into Eve as Adam topped him.

"Shut the hell up, faggot," Adam groaned, coming. "Two and true. Eve, roll over, I have need of your lovely ass."

"You two must be awful bored tending my garden," Eve laughed, her blonde hair a war flag.

Lucifer buried his face in her shampoo'ed tresses, they smelled of cardamom. Adam took her ass, and the Devil and Man fucked Woman -

the way it always is in ménage à trois.

"Look, three fresh apple trees!" Eve exclaimed when they finally awoke from their slumbering pile. It was summer again. "Where did these come from? Adam, you never plant me apples!"

Adam and Lucifer shared a knowing look.

"Let's say I had a friend's help," Adam said, taking Eve's offered fruit and cutting it into lobules with his paring knife.

"Indeed," Lucifer agreed. They ate the temptation seed

and all.

GUTTER-SWILL

Gabriel looked at the crux of Michael's neck. It was a golden scapula, hardened by combat and tan from Machon sun. They had finished battle - thus always to tyrants - and were obsessively polishing their blades of any demon gore, and his brother's green eyes were lucid in clarity - like Eve's pendulous apples, sweet on Gabriel's tongue.

Gabriel studied his reflection in Michael's broadsword: curly dark hair, clear blue eyes, and olive skin with freckles. There was a mole on his right cheek he had always tried to rub away as a cherub, thinking it a speck of dirt as he frolicked with the Seven: Michael, Raphael, Uriel, Gabriel, Zadkiel, Jophiel, and Samael. And oh, how his seven sisters and brothers had been torn apart... Samael remade Lucifer, Zadkiel wandered so far off adrift into Arcturus out of depression, no one could save him, and Jophiel the Herald of Hell, a fallen angel.

Where there had been Seven, now there were Four: Michael, the glue, Raphael, the laughter, Gabriel, the song, and Uriel, the heart.

"It's your birthday, Gabe," Michael said quietly, dressed in his blue and red toga and leather chest plate.

Gabriel quieted: it was the day the ewes gave milk. It was Spring. It was Annunciation. It was time.

He softly smiled. "Are you expecting me to be happy?" Gabriel said tenderly, a glimmer in his eye. "Say, Michael, never expect an expecting Virgin. That doesn't make sense, and cents aren't needed in Heaven - with bricks of gold, we can barter our way to Michael's boat for free."

Michael smirked. "Feeling playful, brother?" He set his sword down and gently sat by Gabriel's side, undoing his back plate in their shared tent.

Gabriel softened, his tight muscles from sparring with Asmodeus - whose cane saber had drawn lacerations all over - making him feel like a hot mess. "Just trying to deal with the itch after our broken bones heal. Say, why do you think Father makes us recreate these battles every day? It's Cold War - our economies, Heaven and Hell, are intertwined - we're partying with Samael in Hell by night, then by day, clocking in the Medieval Times jousting 9 to 5.

We all know it's only for maintaining "balance" - what if we let the world just hang askew?"

"Can't do that," Michael murmured, massaging Gabriel's shoulder. His top was off - Michael always eased his top off without him even noticing. "Mother wouldn't be happy either. She wants her sons and daughters to be warriors."

"Well," Gabriel said pointedly, "FUCK Mom and Dad."

"Hmph," Michael laughed, bemused. He set holy water from his elven palms to work their way into Gabriel's wounds and sores, ease his grinding bones, and bring Baptismal pleasure to a battle-weary warrior. "Buttercream frosting is calling your name. Uriel made us cupcakes. She figured we'd want to take them alone... as we always do on your birthday."

Gabriel's dick tightened, his balls quivered with heat. "Are you my birthday present again, brother?" he said in excitement, his tiresome ways forgotten.

They had camped on a million battlefields - in highland and desert, on island and plain, in snow and in rain. This was a nebulous Black Forest - Samiel's domain - and they had to chain Gabriel's hounds to guard the perimeter of headquarters, their barracks camp.

The hounds bayed as they celebrated Saphael's moon. Michael lowered Gabriel onto his back, Gabriel's brown breeches and leather sandals stained with blood. Michael contemplatively ran his waterbending hands over Gabriel's chest - his nipples plucked to attention, begging to be devoured.

"I'm always your birthday present," Michael winked, his flaming orange hair and emerald eyes bemused. He reached under the cabinet and took out a box of Uriel's perfectly decorated buttercream pumpkin cupcakes with gold foil in the shape of angel wings on them.

Delicately, Michael popped the lid open, then set them on Gabriel's nipples frosting side down.

Gabriel moaned as his hot, hot nipples were coated in cool, soft, buttery textured frosting, the foil melting on his skin.

"Well, that's good, at least my birthdays are predictable," Gabriel sighed, looking at Michael in longing.

Michael's cock twitched under his tunica, poking skyward - the great golden equine rod. Gabriel's own brown cock stirred, and Michael used each hand to minister to them, unzipping their flys, and set to nibbling at the cupcakes, his beautiful berry lips stained with buttercream and pumpkin pie filling.

Gabriel groaned as Michael's tender hand - strong as cables - knit his dick and balls together in serpentine torture. Stroke, caress, lick - his nipples, taint, and family jewels were hot and bothered, and he was thrusting carelessly with abandon into his lover's familiar hand. If Gabriel was the sword, Michael was the sheath. The Messenger Angel always was one to charge recklessly forward as Michael's offensive general, with Raphael running the spies and Uriel on the defense.

Where there had been Seven, fighting the Aberrations of the Void, now... there were four, and Samael and Jophiel and Zadkiel had surrendered to the darkness - so lost. no, it was not

time to mourn.

It was Gabriel's birthday.

Cupcakes finished, they met as lovers with sweet buttercream kisses. Gabriel danced his tongue across the ridge of Michael's burning mouth. He tasted of candied violets, Cabernet Sauvignon, and Uriel's famous cupcakes.

The gold foil wings Uriel had delicately pressed in the kitchen of edible sugar were caught in Micahel's ginger stubble - like little pricklings of fire - and Gabriel laughed, hugging his brother close, and licked them off to crunch the little pearls of wisdom.

"Happy birthday, brother," Michael said sinfully kindly - as if he was hot chocolate. Gabriel shuddered as Michael gently laid him down on their buckskin bed with golden silk sheets and a deerskin hide comforter from Michael hunting Artor's harts. Michael winked, stripping them of their underwear and belts and shoes. "I'm still hungry."

He licked the precum off Gabriel's brown cock and deepthroated, the sphincter of his mouth coiling around the base of his dick. Then, Michael swallowed his balls in a tea bag, shuffling them around and spitting them out.

Gabriel howled in pleasure, burying his hands in his brother lover's copper coils. He shoved Michael's head back on his dick and facefucked him. Michael moaned, rubbing his rod with one hand and groaning - all hard muscle, like Hercules. So tall, even sitting, he dwarfed Gabriel like a blazing star.

Gabriel pounded, pounded, and then came in fructations of bliss. Oh, if only they were free to wander - to elope - to get married. Angels could never marry - they were married to the Throne. He often envied the demons and Adam and Eve for their marriages.

So they had these quiet, feral moments as Gabriel's hounds bayed.

Michael spent himself on Gabriel's feet. Then, with manna at his tongue, Michael licked the fixings of their genitals up, love in his eye for his brother, as if the cum

was like buttercream.

YOUR ONLY DOLL

Samael pours a shot of vodka and kicks the scuffed heels of his boots onto the bar. He yawns obscenely loud, curtain of dark hair fringing his face in shadow. I tense, drawing away from him on my barstool as he leans back, grinning like a feral hound

"What's a doll to do on a cold wretched night like this, love?" he wonders, his dark chocolate voice like silk. With a lazy flick of the wrist, he passes the bottle to me. It slides wildly down, tipping precariously over the edge.

I do nothing. Instead, I glare, my eyes scorpion pincers. The vodka falls, splattering across the cigarette butted-floor.

"You were supposed to catch it, worm."

"I don't drink, Samael," I reply, meeting his smug gaze. The smell of alcohol, repugnant, fills the air.

"Oh, look at you: the virginal embodiment of virtue." He crooks his eyebrow, chuckling darkly. "Oh, wait. Scratch the virginial part. You seem to have lost that as of late-"

"I am going to shove that bottle so far up your demonic!-"

"Now, now, angel: don't let foul words sully your golden tongue." He closes the space between us, his vice-like arms wrapping like a clamp around my waist. The demon of my worst nature smirks, his spicy breath hot in my ear: "There's enough acid on those sweet lips, after all."

I wrench his hands away. Fire flashes in his eyes. "You're disgusting," I say, my voice Arctic cold, at odds with his burning lips.

Samael's smile becomes mocking. "But you like it, little lamb. Admit it. In that beautiful heart of yours lays a mangled, blackened sheep. Jesus is the

Mystical Lamb, but the Whore of Babalon? Why, she is my flock-"

"Shut up!" I snap, blushing furiously. "I've never regretted anything in my life as much as you." My words, venomous, ring through the bar, drawing perplexed looks from my patrons. A pool ball clangs on a table in the silence of the room.

He looks at me witheringly. "You refuse my drink and hand. You can refuse me all you want. But mark my words, dark angel," he hisses. "I will have your soul. Even if there is Hell to pay."

"Hell's not worth what your love would cost me!" I stand up, torn between his burning stare and the cold winter wind beyond the door. Dogs bale in the distance as Longfellow's Great Sammael rides the ghost train of cold, mountain air.

My tempter glowers, taking a shot and pouring himself another- absinthe, by the looks of it. His fingers curl like claws around the glass. "Why..." he muses softly, shattering the glass in his iron grip. He licks the blood from his fingers contemplatively, grinning as I recoil. "...do you put a price on love?"

"Because only a fool follows her heart blindly." I back away slowly, my wiry limbs trembling. Samael rises, his lean hips aligned with my chest, the weight of his presence crushing me. I find myself dazed, somehow beyond the bar, back against the merciless alley wall. Memories of Azazel's touch slice across my mind. I panic, breaths growing ragged, my heart a merciless drum. A flash of concern mars my guardian demon's razor face. He reaches out a hand, brushing my cheek.

His touch is fire.

"You can run from love, but you cannot escape," he whispers, voice like the abyss. "It will hunt you down, half-mad, across the world." He examines my wrist, the tilt of my lips, smiling softly. "Fragile thing. My beautiful, delicate thing..." And then, ever so slow as if savoring my breakability, he takes my hand in his.

I tremble. "Will you break me, Samael?"

He hushes me, murmuring. "All dolls are broken angels. No..."

Silence.

Silence in his heart.

A pause- a breath.

"I'm only here to fix you."

SWEET TOOTH

The kitchen was full of violent delights—chaotic wafts of lemon meringue from the oven, yeasted donut dough rising beside powdered sugar as frying oil simmered in a wok – and a demon hellbent on making his girlfriend Eve the perfect pastries for Valentine's Day.

"How the hell do you make this cottagecore nonsense look so easy?" Samael grunted, dressed in severe black reaping robes as his void tentacles held a box of ingredients – eggs, whole milk, a cup of sugar. Covered in flour over his strawberry covered apron (that belonged to the Mother of Humanity, on loan to her boyfriend), Eve simply giggled, doing homework for Gehenna University.

"It's not that hard to follow instructions, Sammy," Eve clucked, scribbling a derivative about soul economics. Beelzebub had promoted her to Secretary of Pandaemonium. It was a leg up from her decade-long internship that had made her wine and cheese girl of all the demon's corporate events. She'd gotten used to whipping up delicious appetizers in the Hellopolis and it's adjacent offices. A sprinkle of cucumber dill sandwiches. A meringue to please Lucifer. A delightfully arranged charcuterie for Molech. Beelzebub's favorite chocolate torte.

But it was almost Valentine's, and Samael had insisted. So he visited her in the campus dorm.

"So, I mold the dough into a divot with my thumb..." the void demon of death, chaos, misery fussed, pressing the dough. He dolloped the lemon meringue in. Then, ever so gently – as gentle as a clawed, seere black nightmare creature of the utter depths could be – fried the donuts in the clear oil.

Eve's nostrils flared. She was delighted. "Oh Sam, that smells so good! You've gotten to be such a better cook this decade! Remember when you made tacos for the first time? I was only my way back from work and you abducted me with a bag, then locked me in your basement with you in a chef outfit – and you made by-the-box crunchy tacos. The sour cream was expired."

Samael grunted, ignoring his girlfriend. She was a talker. A curvy, luscious, blonde chatterbox. He either choked her or shoved his dick in her mouth when she talked too much. But Eve was kind, and he was harsh, and when he grunted, it sounded like wind through a Roman graveyard, eons old, with legions of dead soldiers hailing the Archangel of Edom.

Enough of that, he thought. This was all for her. The promotion had been hard. A decade ago, it had just been them. No one else to warm her bed. But now, she had Adam, Beelzebub – Lucifer, Molech. Even godsdamned Belial and Asmodeus. Samael had been greedy when he'd stolen her from Lu. Michael was one thing – Eve was born of the twins' flesh, after all.

But these others, cloying the hierodule's bed, siring heirs. Qayin was doing well, it was true – she had the blood of a queen – but these other Nephil brats – they posed a threat.

"Chavah, do you ever think of leaving me?" Samael muttered, powdering the donuts.

"What was that?" Eve sang, draping herself over him. His back spines and raven feathers cluttered her simple human form – no danger there, no sharp edges to cut or foiled flesh to stab – and decorated her like war spoils. "Mmm, you feel so cold. I love it."

He presented her the donuts. "Hot, be careful," Sam said.

They sat down at the kitchen dorm table and waited for them to cool. He helped with her accounting.

"How does Beelzebub do this all day," Eve sighed. "This promotion is so hard."

"He doesn't like to have fun," Samael snorted. He smiled at her, but aches and pains set into his dozen winged, million eyed flesh. "Eve, do you mind, me being death? I'm not pretty like Lucifer. I'm not strong like Michael. I'm not even a god, like Molech. What I am is pain. Hard edges. Don't you want someone glimmering, soft? Why – why do you say, I am your heart? I am your first and last?"

Eve's blue eyes glimmered and she squeezed his tangled hand, the bones shifting and broken, fur and scales. "I like you. Death, it's the most just force in the world. And you – you're the kindest."

They kissed, and it felt like heaven. His suction cup hands danced across her knuckles, she nursed at the black blood at his neck, and he bent her over the desk, and they made love like a Stradivarius string snapping. It was an old, lush dance – as old as Gan Eden – but it was always new, a hymen always to snap, a new way to proclaim: you are my only jewel.

After cleaning up, they feasted. Eve smiled, sitting in his lap.

"Happy Valentine's." Sam smiled, baring shark teeth and a gullet like a Blind God flute. "It's not for a week!" Eve said, teasing.

"Call me a sentimental man." He settled, finally, into his human form. Eve preferred what she had once called monster. Now, it was her favorite type of Samael – the one crooked and broken. The one others thought hideous. But to her, the loam of dead soil, the worms – the abyss and cracked bone – the legions of nightmares and lamia – it was almost like a Paradise, in bustling metropolis Hell.

"I call you mine," Eve said. "You are my first –"
"And last."

When they slept in her tiny bed that night, Samael dreamed of lavender. It smelled like an old grandmother. He could see, eventually, the majesty humans would become – when they too

Were old Cracked

Wise And Broken.

It was comforting. Eve stirred in his arms as he played with her hair.

When they woke in the morning, Eve made challah toast with eggs sunny side up and Manuka honey.

Samael ate. He loved.

Eve smiled. She loved.

And just like that, a new sun rose. And they had leftover donuts.

ABOUT THE AUTHOR

Allister Nelson (she/her) is a multiple Pushcart Prize-nominated author whose work has appeared in The British Fantasy Society, Apex Magazine, ILLUMEN, Eternal Haunted Summer, Renewable Energy World, Frontiers in Health Communication, The National Science Foundation, Luna Station Quarterly, Prismatica Press, Coffin Bell, FunDead Publications, and many other venues. Her work has been translated internationally into Polish and Spanish, and has appeared in anthologies alongside Graham Masterston, Bill Willingham, Jane Yolen, and Alan Dean Foster. By day, she's a D.C.-adjacent Communications and Marketing Nut ("Allie's a Natural Washingtonian: a mile wide and an inch deep"), proud staff writer at Pride With a Bite, and senior technical and science writer. By night, she dabbles in prose, poems, Greco-Roman found feminism graphic novels, and illustrations. In her spare time, Allie is a wanderer of graveyards, weaver of fables, caster of literary aspersions, and gazer at alien starships. She'd like to kiss Mothman one day.